SEA CAMP

A NOVEL BY CHARLES L. RICE

SUN UP PRESS
TUCSON, ARIZONA

This is a work of fiction. Any resemblance to specific persons,
living or dead, is purely coincidental.

SUN UP PRESS • TUCSON, AZ

Cover art reprinted by permission of The Michiganensian,
The 1929 Michigan University Yearbook

"Love After Love" from THE POETRY OF DEREK WALCOTT
1948-2013 by Derek Walcott, selected by Glyn Maxwell.
Copyright © 2014 by Derek Walcott.
Reprinted by permission of Farrar, Straus and Giroux.

Printed in the USA

Names: Rice, Charles L.
Title: Sea Camp | by Charles L. Rice
Description: Young professor goes to the beach for the weekend.
While reminiscing, he considers his religious past and present.
Identifiers: LCCN 2017916506 | ISBN 978-0-692-96850-5
Subjects: Fiction, LGBT, progressive Christian, religion, camp meeting,
carousel, beach towns.

AUTHOR'S NOTE

In 1972, as I began more than 3 decades teaching at Drew University, a representative of a large publishing house in Atlanta made me an offer. The publisher would give me a generous advance—very welcome to a young professor—if I would write a novel "from a Christian perspective." Within a year I had written *Sea Camp* and the editor had cleared it for publication in 1973. But that year the publisher closed its doors. I refunded the advance and the manuscript began 45 years languishing in a desk drawer. The book revived when I came across a letter from a secretary at the publishing house written in 1973. "Dr. Rice, I read your book while preparing it for the editor here. I just wanted you to know that I hope it gets published because you wrote a very good book."

So *Sea Camp* came out of the desk drawer. I found a fine editor and an excellent designer, and here it is, still very much alive, I believe, and relevant to questions of identity, faith, and sexuality. I thank my editor, Kathleen Daley, and a good many careful readers who have helped and encouraged me.

A special thanks goes to the designer of this book and my companion of 42 years, Robert Barker. I thank him for his support and humor through these many years.

CHAPTER

1

North Carolina, 1969

It was only a two-hour drive to Strand Beach, but he was up well before 7:00 for the first time in weeks. The last time must have been the day back in June when Dorie and he had gone to the market earlier than usual and then had driven out into the country to an auction. He had come back with the milking stool that he had refinished and moved from room to room in his teakwood and shag apartment.

He peered through the half-open shutters as he lathered his face. The mists were just rising, and it would be cool until 11:00.

If he had not had other plans, he would have gone for a bike ride on such a morning, when the town was quiet and the breeze that you could make with a bike blew fresh in your face. A bike allowed you to hear the birds and even the radios in the frontside kitchens. Usually he passed the paperboy, and they would wave like conspirators who had in common something more than just being up early or riding bicycles. The last time he had gone riding early down Rolling Road to the park, he had met the milkman going and coming and both times he thought how nice the clinking of bottles sounded as he tried to calculate how much milk he would need to order

1

if he started getting it in bottles on the porch.

It would be a good day for the trip, and maybe Sunday would be good too. He usually shaved after breakfast, but today he wanted to get started and stop for breakfast on the way. He remembered a diner about half way, just beyond where the coastal flats began. From there the road went straight east to the coast. He rubbed his face approvingly and thought that early next week he would take that spin on the bike.

He still missed his old car, "Avis" he called her. He had driven that bug from the time he had come to Collegemont as a graduate student six years ago. Now that he was on the faculty, he could afford the Audi, but he had parted with Avis much more reluctantly than with the graduate school furniture, which by now had been recycled through the College Trading Post to some other student's two rooms. He had even enjoyed his students' cracks about the old car: "Hey Dr. Newall, when are you going to give that to the Smithsonian?" or "Is she on the endangered species list?" But he couldn't help admiring the congruity, as he tossed the duck beach bag into the back seat, between his apricot car and the coral Sans Souci Apartments.

Dorie liked the Audi, and she would have enjoyed the trip. He didn't know why he had not called her to go with him today. And he was sure that the question would occur to her. Even now he could wake her up and she would probably go. But he drove past the cluster of phone booths by Sharp's Drug and continued down Main Street.

The sun was in his eyes until he passed the business district, which was just beginning to stir as Joe put out the newspaper racks and Early's opened for breakfast. He passed the Presbyterian Church, realizing that he had forgotten all about the morning paper which must still be on the front porch.

He skirted the edge of campus where the oak trees arched over the street. He ducked his head to look up toward the window of his office on the second floor of Brown Hall. He took pleasure in the fact that his department was in the old red brick building in the oldest part of campus. His office had Gothic windows and a big oak door with a plastic nameplate stamped: SCRIBER NEWALL, HISTORY.

Then he was going downhill into the sun, headed out past the shopping center and the bowling alley that had been turned into some kind of bar and restaurant. He was on his way toward Rikesville and the coast. A mileage sign advised, "Edenstown 49." He would stop there to eat.

Since coming down from the North he had been fascinated by small Southern towns and back roads. He and Dorie had spent several Saturdays "shunpiking," a word he had learned from *Southern Living*. Dorie liked to browse in antique shops, and he had once found a brass lamp that seemed to fit well enough with his other furnishings.

He followed old Route 96 (there was now a four-lane highway with the same number) that skirted the contours of the Piedmont hills and made the sharper turns necessary to avoid the best farmland or to miss the farmhouses that had been there before pavement. He recalled that the road even veered around a big oak tree, just outside Rikesville. It occurred to him that it was the perfect place for one of those signs about preparing to meet God.

Rikesville seemed a hundred miles and years away

from Collegemont. The new highway, which had cut the actual distance from the University to twenty-one miles, bypassed Rikesville altogether. You had to be going there to go there, and if you did go through the old town, old Route 96 became a modest avenue bordered by white houses with long front porches and shaded lawns. Some of the houses had turrets that made him wonder what their round rooms must look like, undoubtedly as strange and inaccessible to him as the lives of the people who lived here and periodically sent their shy children to University, not altogether happy but nevertheless proud to be doing so.

The road ran straight up to the white brick courthouse and around it to the other side of Rikesville where some of the black residents were walking toward the courthouse or sitting on little shed porches that came right to the sidewalks.

A sign advised "Resume Safe Speed." He was getting hungry. He turned on the radio out of habit. Southern radio stations all sounded alike once he was beyond the range of WUCM-FM, the college radio station. The first thing he noticed was that in the South they advertised grocery prices on the radio. Was there any other part of the country where they did that? Out in Iowa or Texas? And down here you could hear a sermon at just about any hour of the day or night. He avoided the sermons and took the only other option, a nasal singer with a down-home accent: "No such thing as a broken heart . . . ." He turned it off after a while. It was not that he did not appreciate local color. In fact, he had written his dissertation on "The Historical Sources of Josiah Royce's Concept of Provincialism," and since then had grown increasingly out-

spoken in his classroom and elsewhere about the homogeniz-
ing of American life and the reduction of everything to what
Royce had called a "harassed dead level of mediocrity." He
was glad that every station in the country did not sound like
New York or WUCM-FM. But it was a bit early in the morning for sampling the county's distinctive flavor.

There weren't many billboards, only an occasional
automobile dealer's sign or a barn with one side painted
black and yellow, advertising chewing tobacco or fertilizer.
A church turned up about every three miles, some of them
down at the heels, but most had a decent coat of paint and
more often than not a cemetery that looked cared for. He
liked to see a well-kept church. It would be nice to drive along
here on Sunday morning and hear all those bells. You could
probably hear one after another if they all started at 11:00 or
so. But he hoped to be out on the beach soaking up the sun at
11 a.m. tomorrow.

He kept thinking that it was unusual for him to be going off by himself like this. The summer crowd around campus was small and congenial—a good many people had gone
off to Europe—and he could easily have found someone to
go along, even a foursome. Todd had suggested several times
that they go off to the beach together. It wasn't that he had decided not to ask Todd or Dorie. He had seen them both at the
pool Friday afternoon. Something had just kept him from taking any initiative. And when the usual week-end invitations
came, for a cookout at the lake or for brunch on Sunday, he
had pleaded the need to finish something that he was writing.
And he hadn't really been sure until he threw the bag in the
car that he was going at all, to say nothing of going alone.

He had had a great time this summer. He had been getting up without the alarm clock and spending the morning reading and writing. He was working on an article for a quarterly review piece, a chapter gleaned from his dissertation, which he hoped would get popular attention. A brief article in the local paper last spring had sparked his imagination when he read that people had begun moving out of California and back east, to Oklahoma and the Midwest and all the other places from which they had migrated by the millions since the '30s. He was interested in the phenomenon of people trying to get back to their roots, and he was trying to show how Royce had been a prophet when he resisted the whole idea of the melting pot and encouraged people to keep their ties with their own past and their own places. He was pretty sure that he could finish the article in a few more mornings, certainly before the new term begins week after next.

Afternoons he assigned several hours to reading for his new course on "Freedom and Loyalty in the American Tradition," and, when the weather was good, swimming in the University's pool. In the evening he could go to one of those dinner parties that always began with something to drink on the screened porch or the patio and moved toward cold supper or cookouts, then dancing or listening to music stretched out on the living room floor.

This was, as he thought about it, the first time he had been really alone this summer, out of reach of the telephone and away from his work, which lay in neat stacks of index cards and scribbled yellow sheets on the desk in his bedroom.

CHAPTER

2

WELCOME TO EDENSTOWN
LIONS MEET TUESDAY
GRACIE'S RESTAURANT

It had been a year since he and Dorie had followed up on an advertisement she had clipped out of the paper and taken a Sunday tour of Edenstown. It had reminded him of where he had grown up, and he suddenly realized that he looked forward to returning.

The countryside was flattening out now, and the highway made one long curve down into the town before it became Main Street. You couldn't get lost in Edenstown anymore than you could in Lincoln, Oklahoma. The streets were north or south of Main Street and numbered like ribs: First, Second, Third. . . . (He had grown up on South Eighth Street in Lincoln less than two blocks from his father's drug store where he had worked at the soda fountain in the summer.) At the corner of Sixth and Main an arrow pointed north to "Edenstown Baptist Church, One Block." He might take time some day to see if that church looked like the one on Sixth Street in Lincoln—red brick with a false façade, starved shrubbery and a sign out front that had been repainted for as long as he could remember with the same words: "We Preach

Christ" just above the minister's name, which was the only part of the sign that ever changed.

One image from his boyhood was indelible in his memory, the worn pews in his grandmother's church. The dark varnish had been worn off the tops of the pews. He learned even as a boy how that had happened. On communion Sundays, after she had received the little cube of bread and put the "shot glass" in the holder on the back of the pew, she would bend way over, bow her head to the top of the pew, and hold on with both hands.

He used to sit with his hands folded during the sermon and wonder. How many years had people held on to those pews, or rubbed them with their heads, like his grandmother did? It must have taken decades to wear through the dark varnish like that. They probably didn't have those old pews anymore, or if they did, they had re-varnished them by now. He had mentioned it to Dorie, who had laughed and said: "Can you imagine taking the varnish off of a whole church full of furniture? It took us months just to do that old trunk in my bedroom."

Gracie's Restaurant was a new place, just beyond the last gas station as you left town going east. There were a couple of trucks parked near the road and a dozen cars nosed up to the picture windows with their gold curtains pulled back like a schoolgirl's hair.

The construction workers, and most of the truck drivers, had had breakfast by now. These cars belonged to salesmen or local businessmen who didn't open up before 9:00. He took a seat at the counter beside two men in slacks and perma-press shirts. Paper mats with a map of the state featured a big star where Gracie's Restaurant would be. The coffee cup was already in place, with a rider of half-and-half already set up. A waitress was pouring coffee at the tables, and when she came to the counter, she filled his neighbors' cups without speaking.

"Coffee?" she asked. He was an outsider.

"Yes, please."

"Menu?"

"No, just give me ham and scrambled eggs with whole wheat toast. Some of that country ham if you have it, and grapefruit juice."

"We got country ham but we ain't got no brown bread. Just white. OK?"

He nodded.

"Paper's over there," she said, and walked to the kitchen, writing on the green pad. He could hear her say as she pushed the swinging door with her hip, "Two scrambled with ham what am." In New York it would have been "wreck 'em" and they would have had whole wheat bread.

His coffee was still hot when he came back from the men's room, and a sweating glass of juice was waiting. He wouldn't look at the paper just now.

He had been interested in the bathroom graffiti, scrawled on the wall where anyone over five feet tall couldn't miss it, and anyone under that would have to stand on tiptoe to read it. There were telephone numbers, and dates and hours that had come and gone. And there were the usual poems and the drawings done hurriedly and without a model (unless the artist sketched a self-portrait). Was there a town in America so small, innocent enough to have a men's room without scatological poetry and line drawings? Edenstown was certainly no exception.

He had noticed something else scratched up there. He had become accustomed to the new competition—between the poets and artists on one side and the evangelists on the other. More frequently these days, admonitions to "Repent" appeared along with the assurance that Jesus would save the people who wrote and read such obscenities. He had even seen the Bible quoted alongside less quotable but nonetheless memorable inscriptions, and the quotations were always—at least the ones he had seen—"heavy," as they say. "Repent and believe the gospel" or "the wages of sin is death"—verses that he knew from more than one summer in Vacation Bible School. But he had seen something new today, penciled in a small, neat hand: "Jesus Want Make You Love Sea Camp Sunday." He tried to picture the person, knowing that the door might open at any second, standing close to the wall in that cool, damp room, writing on the wall with a yellow pencil, omitting half of the infinitive and all the punctuation, like someone short of time or money sending an urgent telegram.

He thought, as he downed the grapefruit juice as if he really didn't like it and wanted to get rid of it, that it was a wonder he saw it at all. He was likely to avoid a sentence that began with "Jesus," especially if it were written above a urinal. He doubted that even Jesus would be much pleased with so gross a violation of the conventions of contextual appropriateness, to say nothing of taste.

Somewhere in the Bible was an admonition to avoid casting pearls before swine. Scriber hadn't been going to church, but he still wasn't comfortable when words like "God" or "Jesus"—were there any words like those?—were used to season conversation, like parsley on eggs. It was, he thought, more than just prudery. He had, on one occasion, gotten into the swing of things with the poolside gang and salted his speech. It had sounded strange to him, even ludicrous, as if his great aunt were to wear peddle-pushers downtown. Maybe it was just the bad usage that bothered him.

Gracie's breakfast was good, and he ate quickly. He would be at Strand Beach by the time the sun was hot. (He would have to stop and get some suntan oil. He had left his by the pool at Todd's place).

He had eaten everything on the plate, including the white toast. He would have to go out to breakfast more often. Getting out early made one hungry. It was too easy to settle for toast and coffee with the newspaper and go straight from that to the desk piled with books and journals and scribbled sheets.

He remembered those breakfasts out in Oklahoma and how the days started as if they were going somewhere and you had better get yourself ready before you tried to live through one. They didn't have ham cured like at Gracie's; it was sweeter and thicker, with cream gravy and those biscuits, brown and crusty on top and bottom, as big as the saucer in which his grandfather cooled his coffee. The butter was fresh, as was the wild honey his grandfather had stolen from the bees.

Even after his grandmother got a gas stove fed by a silver tank by the cellar door, she used the old wood-burning "Home Comfort" for all the baking. When his grandfather reminded her one more time that the "new-fangled" stove might not heat up the kitchen so much when summer came, and they could get rid of the wood-burner, she bridled. "I can't make biscuits without a wood stove any more than you can keep your pants up without suspenders, and you would be the first to complain if I made those little hard rocks that some people call biscuits," she would say to him, both of them quietly laughing.

Breakfast was a big thing in his grandparents' house. It seemed to satisfy more than the accumulated hunger of the night, though it certainly did that. Sitting by the double windows in the long kitchen that ran all the way across the back of the old house, they could look down past the barn to the fields where the guinea hens hid their nests and were now telling the whole world about it, and on down to Lead Cow Creek which ran through a long line of cottonwoods and offered a few holes deep enough for swimming on a hot summer day. His grandfather, Abbie, had hung an old tire on a rope and slung it over an overhanging oak tree branch so that he and his brother and their cousins could swing out and drop into the deep water.

Living with his grandparents, before his family had moved to a house in town, they got a newspaper, *The Cherokee County Defender*, once a week. It seemed to last that long and was always there at breakfast. The obituaries and the classified section played a large role in the morning ritual. Whose place was for sale and why? Who had died? How were they related to us? Did they have any land, and where were their children now? It was as if the day could not begin until the family had placed itself in relation to the dead and the living.

Scriber hadn't thought about this ritual for a long time.

One morning they were going through the paper, reading about deaths and births and marriages. (He was at his grandparents for breakfast that day as he often was in the spring when they needed him on the farm). His grandmother, Nina, had asked him to fill the sugar bowl and he had scooped out of the salt canister. When his grandfather had sugared and creamed and buttered his oatmeal, he took a big spoonful and looked first at her and then at the boy, first with disbelief and then with great heavy tears in his eyes that seemed not to want to run down his face. He poured the oatmeal into the bucket that was for the pigs and then, without turning around, said that he had forgotten that today was April 1. I was never sure whether the old man had believed him when he told him, then and later, that he didn't know it was that day. But the times they spent together out on the farm told him that he was forgiven.

Those breakfasts were daily feasts, long past from these days when a newspaper was fresh, the bread old, and married people launched themselves out into a day as if it were nothing at all to live through another one.

"No more coffee, thank you." The waitress had been filling up his cup while he ate.

It probably didn't take long to become a regular at Gracie's. He was sure that if he had said the first word, she would have stood with the glass pot in one hand and an ample hip in the other, talking about prospects for good weather at the beach or what a pretty orange car he had.

She had undoubtedly seen him drive up, a thirty-four-year-old college type in a short-sleeved sweatshirt with the college logo emblazoned on the front, and tight faded jeans. He stood out, appearing taller than his six feet, leaner than most men his age.

He put two quarters near his plate, paid the man reading the paper at the cash register and left Gracie's, hoping for as good a breakfast at the Holiday Inn tomorrow.

CHAPTER

3

The highway forks just east of Edenstown. Old 96 angles southeast and the other road goes north to the newer and, at that time, more popular resorts.

He, Todd and Dorie had gone up to Ocean City, Maryland, last summer, where the boardwalk was new and there were chic shops right by the beach. A little hole-in-the-wall printing shop there could produce almost anything you wanted. Todd and Dorie had bought him an early birthday present. He still had a supply of the calling cards they had given him: "Scriber Newall—Stud Professor."

He was glad to follow the older two-lane road—new to him—taking in the rolling farmland. On another day he would probably have picked up the hitchhiker. But today, as he had told Dorie, he needed to be alone, for some reason not yet clear.

He saw the boy at a distance. He concluded right away that he was a student headed for the beach. Coming closer, Scriber saw his small shirt-board sign that read "Sea Camp."

The boy's easy slouch said that he did not have the weight of the world on those broad shoulders. Not quite as tall as the professor—typical of students he saw often at the gym, stocky and muscular—but with what Todd called "kitten hips." His only luggage was a flight bag suggesting a week-end in a swimsuit. As the Audi passed him, he gave Scriber a friendly look that was almost recognition, as if they had something in common. It was to Scriber all the more surprising that he passed the boy by, intriguing as he now seemed. But hitchhikers are strangers and strangers feel constrained to talk in a car and that is not what he wanted today.

As he watched the slim figure recede in the mirror, the boy gave him a small wave that was somehow friendly. Scriber almost touched the brake but drove on, harboring the possibility that he might see the fellow again.

The two-lane road was straight now, and it would reach the coast in less than an hour. He wouldn't hurry. There was no need to arrive at the motel before they had the room ready, and the sun wouldn't be hot until eleven. He would have time to swim before lunch.

He had more to observe of the countryside. The land looked sandy, the kind of soil that is good for watermelons and peanuts, and in the old days, cotton. There were a few fields of soybeans. He recognized them as the same plants Walter Cronkite had shown last week on the news. A reporter had interviewed someone at State College and the expert had said that we could produce enough high-class protein for everyone if we stopped feeding soybeans to livestock and converted grazing land to growing soybeans for ourselves. All we needed was to get used to the idea, but this expert was not optimistic, it had seemed, about the possibility of weaning Americans from steak and roast beef. Food practices, he said, are as deeply ingrained as religion.

The farms had undoubtedly once been more prosperous, probably in the days when cotton was the major product of these flat fields. Now, some of the houses appeared to be larger than the occupants could afford to paint. The one he was approaching was big enough for a family as large as the one in which his father grew up with three brothers and four sisters. Probably only an old couple lived there now, their children long since moved to the city. Did it hold the texture of a Saturday morning, of a quietly ticking clock that sounded loud in a big house where not much was happening but where a great deal had happened? Where its owners were going about doing the necessary things, remembering more than they were looking forward to?

The flowers in the yard were the kind that a farm-woman would plant: hollyhocks, petunias, and patches of sea thrift running down the bank to the road where the mailbox had its red flag up. Up by the porch was half of a hot water heater that the old man had probably painted silver and in which the old woman had planted red geraniums. Over to one side of the walk was a plaster of Paris hen with her chalky chicks, maybe a present brought by the families whose station wagons and children filled the yard on Sunday afternoons and Mother's Days.

Scriber thought how quiet the place would be on a Sunday morning when the old couple had gone off to a church either up or down the road.

He wondered if people came from this far away to sell their produce at the farmers' market in Collegemont. The market was in the old armory, on the side of town he saw no more often than weekly. He hadn't even been aware of the place during his student years when he consumed food with little thought about its source or quality.

A few stalls were open on Tuesdays and Thursdays, but the main event was on Saturday, from about the middle of May until the last pumpkins and chrysanthemums of October or November. He was just finishing his first year on the faculty when someone mentioned it, but it had been June before he got there, with Dorie.

She called late one Friday to say that she would come by early Saturday. They arrived by 7:00, he with his face barely washed and Dorie looking fresh, with a canvas shopping bag on her arm that had a picture of a pine tree and the words "Save a Tree." They had bought squash and beans and what the woman called "mixed greens." He found a lady selling cakes and canned things and went home with pound cake and scuppernong jelly at which Dorie, who was into organic cooking, smiled indulgently. They bought big brown eggs—Dorie had a used empty egg carton in the bag which the man filled—and flowers. Back at his apartment, while Dorie tried to arrange the gladiolus which were too tall for the vase and the apartment, he cooked breakfast.

He had thought at first that it was no more than the fresh eggs that made him look forward to the Saturdays that followed. As the summer went along, the market grew increasingly rich and colorful. Tomatoes and berries and zucchini joined cantaloupes and watermelons and fresh peas of all kinds that they would shell while watching television or just talking on the deck. The flowers seemed to flourish, and he was able to enjoy flamboyant zinnias, his favorite, every week. And he enjoyed the quiet ways and obvious pride of the farmers as they displayed their produce.

The men wore overalls or khakis and sported honest suntans; their wives, big-boned and fresh-faced, probably worked out of doors also but wore bonnets against the sun.

Occasionally he would meet a colleague or a student and they would speak in passing but these exchanges were seldom long enough to be called conversations. The market had its own liturgy, a pattern governed by the necessity of meeting real and elemental human needs. Personal intercourse was casual but honest, thus unusual. One was constantly elbowed and jostled, giving the unmistakable sensation of being with people. But at the same time there was the anonymity of routine, marked out by the necessity of getting on with it and going home for breakfast. A profound economy of motion and speech prevailed which was, at the same time, as casual as the seeming indifference with which the farmers' wives weighed green beans on the hanging scales, always throwing on a few more for good measure.

Over a period of time, he had developed his own pattern, calling first at his favorite stalls and then going up one aisle and down another. No antisepsis of the supermarket here. Human hands had touched everything in the buying and selling, and the language of asking and giving—abbreviated, full of trust and goodwill—would have made a mockery of piped-in music.

The woman he bought most of his vegetables from told him that she and her husband—who wore starched overalls and hardly spoke a word—got up at 4:30 on Saturday mornings. She always wore pastel dresses that looked like they had just been ironed, and you could tell by looking at her that the next morning she would be up early to get dinner ready before going off to her Sunday school class, that was likely named for Dorcas or Mary Martha or some other biblical woman. He had guessed that they went to bed on Friday night at 8:30 or 9:00 after they had the pickup loaded, or maybe they just sat out on the porch until later, not talking, not needing to. He couldn't imagine that farm woman watching the late show on television.

He remembered the day when she had put a few more well-scrubbed new potatoes in the bag which already weighed a pound, and he had said, remembering his grandmother, "That's good Methodist measure." She had smiled in such a way that he knew he had inadvertently touched her essence, though she would not have mentioned it there weighing out beans and potatoes.

One day her son, a bronzed young farmer about Scriber's age, had been there to help when the big pumpkins were coming in. He noticed how the man, who was going grey, called her "Mama" and the peaceful man, "Daddy."

Scriber hardly missed a summer Saturday at the market, and he often came home with far more vegetables than he could eat and with as many flowers. Now beginning a weekend at the beach, he realized that he was already missing the lady in the pastel dress and wondered again if the people in that house back there might go as far as Collegemont to sell produce.

CHAPTER

4

The towns along here were no more than villages. The smallest had at least two churches and a few stores with fake facades and long shady porches. He had hardly slowed to 35 mph before he was back on the open highway driving between fields of peanuts. He stopped at a large building with "Planters" painted on the side, but was told that they didn't sell peanuts there. He would have to buy them at the store in the next town. He guessed that they would be like those dehydrated facsimiles that everyone was serving before dinner. "Peanuts, peanuts, everywhere," he said out loud, making a gesture towards the sandy fields.

The car that passed him was not really going fast. It was just that his pace was already that of a stroller on the beach. The hitchhiker had got a ride with four other tousled young people in a Volkswagen. They were talking animatedly, but there was no question that the young man recognized the apricot car with its lone driver. The glance he gave Scriber was not unfriendly or accusing, merely inquisitive. The van bus was the color of a field mouse and had a sticker on the rear bumper: "Honk if You Love Jesus." The Volkswagen was almost out of sight when Scriber speeded up a little.

The first signs of the beach towns began to appear.

He passed a motel advertising "$6 Single, $9 Double," one of those old places with a dozen or so doors opening off of one long porch, like a cloister. The doors had been painted different colors, and, judging by the number of cars, about half of the rooms were occupied. Monks would have been up long ago, walking up and down saying their morning prayers. He tried to imagine the people sleeping behind the blue and red and yellow doors and what "morning obligation" would mean to them.

It was quite surprising how often he thought of monasteries and monks. Ever since that Sunday at the Cloisters Museum in New York—or perhaps the deepest impression had come when he took the train from Paris to Chartres and walked up the hill like some pilgrim until he stood before the Cathedral—he had found himself wondering what it was really like, living away from things with a group of people who did something together besides talk most of the time. Sometimes when he was caught in traffic, he would turn off the radio and think about cloisters with their cool stone floors and wrap-around courtyards, or he would remember that day going out to Chartres.

He had seen cathedrals before; he even had slides of some out-of-the-way ones like Reims and Laon. Perhaps it was taking the train that had made the difference, approaching the town at an appropriate pace. He had brought nothing to read and had regretted that at first because it appeared that there would be nothing to look at but the forest which had hedged the tracks since leaving Paris. He leaned his head against the window and looked far ahead, not searching for anything in particular, enjoying the rocking motion and the train's sounds. The trees began to thin, and he caught glimpses of farms. By the time the train neared Chartres, wide open fields, some yellow now with mustard, and random copses marking streams and fence rows appeared. The train followed a long curve and suddenly a small town was visible on a hill topped by the cathedral, which disappeared as quickly as it had come into view.

When he stepped from the train, he had to ask the way, "En haut, monsieur?" So he had kept going uphill, through the narrow streets and a noisy market where women were selling live chickens and ducks and flowers that he recognized. He was sure, when he got there, that it would not have been the same if he had driven up to the square like a tourist, parking his car in front of a motel room.

He had not even taken his camera to Chartres. In the confused discussion about whether Maxime, the young French policeman who was his host, should drive him to Chartres, he had left it behind. Maxime, who had shown him a good bit of Paris, had decided he did not feel like making the drive, and Scriber had run off to the station at the last minute.

Leaving the camera seemed to him, in retrospect, as propitious as taking the train. The tourist he had watched from a shaded bench at one corner of the cathedral's apron had remembered to bring his Kodak Brownie. The wife and children were on the steps, under the serene composure of the great portal, while the man in plaid shorts, his eye to the lens, was backing across the plaza. He turned the camera one way and then the other, retreating all the while as the family tried to hold the pose as well as the sculpted figures above them did. At the far end of the square, near the shaded benches, the amateur photographer snapped the picture. As he walked back toward the dismissed group, he called out, "Gotcha!"

Scriber had walked down the hill, glad to be sans camera. The next time he might want some colored slides; he wasn't sure. For the moment, he thought, Kodaks and cathedrals seemed incompatible. Had he played the tourist, he might not be able to project himself, even now, back to the immense serenity of that sacred inventory of all things human in cold stone under soaring vaults and burning windows.

CHAPTER

5

The beach towns, except for Sea Camp, were organized for the automobile. He had seen the red and green billboard for the Holiday Inn already, telling him to turn right at the third light and then to do the same thing again. He could, if he wished, live on wheels here. The road was lined with hamburger heavens. They had not gone to soybeans yet. Pizza palaces were thriving, and a smiling pink pig announced the best bar-be-cue anywhere.

The main street of Strand Beach was four lanes wide, and the traffic islands were covered with grass-green carpet. On each side of the street widely-spaced fledgling trees—water oaks he thought—were making some headway in relieving the stretches of concrete. Some of the stores had remodeled fronts, and the parking meters were new.

His hotel was on the beach where the boardwalk narrowed to a mere sidewalk, with the office and entrance to the restaurant on the landward side. He turned off Coke Street and parked under a canopy, noticing for the first time that the big neon sign was actually a stylized star.

The clock behind the desk said 11:00. Both of the clerks were at the teletype, and it was half a minute before the girl, who couldn't have been out of high school, saw him.

"Good morning. Room number?" She thought he was checking out.

"I'm just arriving. I have a reservation, came early for the sun." The other clerk, who also looked like he had just graduated from Strand Beach High, glanced over his shoulder.

"Oh, sure," she said, "that's fine. Name, please."

She found a room that had been made up and said that it was on the ocean side and that it looked like it would be a fine day.

"You can park on the south side. It's not far from your room, 306."

She gave him the key and, without looking at him, said, "Have a nice day."

She had that fresh-off-the-farm look of the freshman girls in his Western Civilization class. At the same time she was businesslike and had already perfected a kind of distancing efficiency and the sort of straightforward friendliness that forbids anything more.

The boy was still bending over the machine as Scriber took the key and left, giving the lobby a quick glance which told him that it was indeed a Holiday Inn, the restaurant in the usual place and a swimming pool through the glass doors at the back. He tried to estimate the age of the place; he had heard that Inn owners tried to dispose of a property after twenty years.

The door to 306 opened off of a walkway that overlooked the pool. As he put the key in the lock, he counted five people stretched out in oily oblivion on white plastic lounge chairs that would leave them striped when they got up. No one was in the water, and the pool attendant, a young man in his twenties, was just carrying away his equipment. The vacuum was obviously heavy, but he walked with squared shoulders and the easy gait of a basketball player dribbling slowly down an empty court.

The room was like any other, except that at the far end were sliding glass doors opening onto a private balcony. The coral-colored curtains were open, and for a moment he had the sensation of being on a ship. He could see a narrow strip of the beach and beyond, blue sea and sky. A few white clouds, no larger than his hand, glided high above. The blue of the sky deepened as it reached the sea, and white sails seemed to reflect the scudding clouds.

He sat on the bed for a moment and then began taking off his shoes. He hadn't seen himself full length for a long time. The only mirror in his apartment was on the door to the middle cabinet, and even Dorie's did not have one full length. It would not occur to him to go out and buy a long mirror. But the one in the imitation marble bathroom was as tall as he was.

He wasn't sure that the phrase "well-preserved" applied to a man not yet halfway to three-score-and-ten, but it was the first to come to mind as he stood there looking at himself, tan already in the blue shorts with white piping. He was well preserved, trim but not skinny for his six feet, and only he could tell that his hair was thinning a bit. His chest and shoulders had once been larger, but he had been told that he could expect to lose a little weight—or to gain a lot—as he moved through the thirties. He might do a few more pushups to tighten up, but he really didn't mind that he was taking on a somewhat more ascetic look, despite the fact that the sportcoat he wore to teach in, the tweedy one with leather patches on the sleeves, was feeling a little large on him. He smiled at himself—good teeth too—and thought of those Charles Atlas ads as he fished his sunglasses and an old tube of suntan cream—he had forgotten to buy some—out of the duck bag and left the room. The oily people by the pool had not moved.

CHAPTER

6

Dorie Foyler woke up early and lay back against the pillows, as she watched the white curtains move in the breeze that would die by nine o'clock. Her parents were coming today and she wondered how it would be this time. From the day she had started college they had come to visit at least twice a year. Her new job as assistant dean of women at the university had not changed that pattern, except that they could stay in her apartment now instead of at the College Inn.

One of the worst visits had been during her sophomore year at Whitfield College. She smiled to herself now as she looked back on it. It was October, her eleventh month at the college and her parents' third visit. Her mother had mentioned—her mother had a way of mentioning which amounted to an ultimatum—that it would be nice to go to the college chapel.

"I believe you have an interesting young chaplain."

On previous parental visits they had gone to the Episcopal church at the edge of the campus. Dorie had been unable to introduce her parents to anyone there except for the young vicar who was around the student center quite a lot. Her parents had assumed—or perhaps she had said so—that she attended the college chapel.

Dorie replied, "We could go to your church. The Presbyterian Church is not far from campus."

They had both noticed that she had called it "your church," and she was in fact a little surprised that she had put it that way. She had, after all, grown up going to the small frame church around the corner from the Baptist church in Tabor City, North Carolina, and on the second Sunday at Whitfield she had stood with several other young women in hats and gloves to join the Presbyterian Church. But after the first semester she had hardly been to church, despite the fact that Mr. Freling had called at her dormitory twice last spring.

It wasn't that she had not thought about the matter. Some Sunday mornings she would hear the church bells and begin to think about what she would wear to church even before it occurred to her that she was not going. It would be nice to wear a cool spring dress and after church walk up Main Street before lunch. Sunday could be such an ordered day, when the chaos of a week on campus and living in a dormitory were held at bay for another hour or two by Presbyterianism. Her father had a favorite phrase, from the Bible, she thought, "everything decently and in order," and it seemed to her that she had never heard a Presbyterian sermon or eaten a Sunday dinner at her mother's table which did not conform to that prescription. Whenever she saw neatly clipped lawns with nothing overdone but everything done, she was sure that there was a Presbyterian not far away. Even now, as she lay watching the movement of the curtains which her mother had made, she felt the attraction of that ordered life, inseparable from the white frame church and decorous Sunday manners.

They had, at her mother's persistence, gone to the college chapel. She had called the student center to make sure of the time and that the service would be held in that small room with an altar on wheels and movable chairs which she had peeked into one day when she was looking for the campus art gallery. The service was at 10:30, and there would be coffee afterwards. She hoped someone would be there whom she knew, and that those who did know her would not make their welcome too effusive. She had seen the chaplain around the campus, a rather fey young man who wore turtle-necks and striped trousers, but she wasn't sure that he knew her name.

It was a fine October morning, cool enough for her new brown suit. Her mother had taken her to Richmond in early summer, and she had come home with what her mother called a fall "outfit," as color-coordinated as an interior decorator's dream. She could see approval and self-satisfaction in her mother's eyes when she came down to find them waiting in one of the small sitting rooms off the dormitory parlor. Her father, too, looked up from his paper to admire his blonde and demure daughter. Sunday was beginning decently and in order.

"Is the chaplain a good preacher?" her father had asked as they followed the brick walk that led diagonally from the dormitories to the administration building.

"I'm no judge of sermons, daddy, I'll leave that to you. He seems to be a nice person, though you may find his style different from Mr. McFarland's." She noticed a few students walking toward Edwards Hall, but they didn't seem to be

31

dressed for chapel.

They were early. She could tell, as soon as they entered the room, that her mother thought they must be in the wrong place, or at least hoped they were. Even before the students in jeans and the chaplain in slacks and a floral shirt arrived, she had felt that they were over-dressed: her mother in a beige suit and peach-colored hat, her father in his regular Sunday blues, and she in a suit which had hardly been seen on the campus since she came.

Two rows of folding chairs were arranged in a circle around the altar, which had been wheeled to the center of the room. She wished they had gone to the Presbyterian Church, but they took three chairs against the wall and waited. By 10:40 about fifty people had come in. The only man besides her father wearing a suit was a young professor who seemed equally new to the place. Everyone else was in sweatshirts and sweaters, and several people sat on the floor. There were no hymn books, just some mimeographed sheets of songs which were being handed out by a young woman wearing a red bandana, who later played the guitar and led the songs. Her parents didn't sing, and even she had more trouble with the tunes than with Scottish plainsong.

The sermon was about civil rights, to which just about everyone answered with "right on," which Dorie took to mean "amen." She thought she had heard the young black man sitting next to her father say, "Yes, that's right" when Mr. Ames, the chaplain, had contended that liberal white churches had thought of themselves too long as the savior of the blacks and that in fact the black churches could teach the whites a few things about how to live and even about how to worship. Everyone, he went on, had something to gain by bringing black and white together, by "breaking down the walls of partition," but that the "uptight" whites probably stood to gain the most. Dorie couldn't tell whether her father's alternate staring at the floor and glancing at her was accusation or sheer discomfort.

Communion followed, a loaf of bread passed from hand to hand, crumbs falling on the red carpet. She knew that her mother had noticed them and that her father's phrase ("everything decently and in order") was running through all three Foyler heads like tickertape. Then they sang a song about how you could know a Christian by his love and passed around a pottery goblet of rosé wine. It had been hard enough for her parents at St. Mark's Episcopal where the priest had wiped the chalice with a clean white cloth. Here, the goblet went all the way around the first row and reached them wet around the rim. When the black student gave the cup to her father with the words which the chaplain had asked them all to use, "The blood of Christ, brother," he had said, "Thank you." If he drank the wine, it was very little, and her mother had passed the cup quickly to her without a word.

As the service was ending, the chaplain hugged the girl with the guitar and everyone was supposed to do the same to his or her neighbor. Dorie said "Good morning" to the girl on her right, who squeezed her shoulder, and her father shook hands with his black neighbor.

"You never know what they are going to do in college chapels these days," Dorie ventured as they walked to lunch. It was a feeble effort. She knew that they knew she had never been to the college chapel before today. She wondered why it mattered to her: why was it so important to conceal the fact from them? They had been as unwilling to confront her as she was to tell them straight out. That had always been their way.

They had gone back to Tabor City soon after lunch and the matter had not come up again, though she hoped that some day they would share a good laugh about it.

On their spring visit that same year, they went to the Presbyterian Church, and when she transferred to the University the following September, they took to coming on Friday evening and returning home on Saturday.

Once she joined the staff of the University and her father had retired from the hardware store, they came when it was convenient for her. So when Scriber had mentioned wanting to get away by himself, she had called to invite them. (She had heard her mother, her hand only partially covering the receiver, say, "Dorie wants us to visit her this weekend," pleasure obvious in her voice.)

She scooted her feet across the nubby rug that her grandmother had hooked and given to her when she moved here. She could feel the breeze, and for a moment she missed Scriber. They would have been going to the market or bicycling down Rolling Road to the park along Sparrow's Creek. He loved the morning, for work and play, and disliked staying up late. If she knew him, he was already on his way to the beach, maybe even there by now.

She had known Scriber for more than two years now. They had met in the summer, in June. He had passed her on his bike twice before he slowed down one day to ride along-side. There were no cars out that early, and they had the street to themselves.

"You must ride this way often?"

There was a question in his voice, and she had felt completely free to tell him that she rode that way just about every day that the weather was good. They rode a mile or so together, and the next day they rode to the coffee shop off the bypass and had breakfast. By the end of the summer they were seeing each other regularly, and more often than not, when he was not eager to get back to his writing, they had breakfast out on the deck at her place. On some days that summer they would ride in the morning, swim in the afternoon, and spend the evening listening to records or just sitting out on his screened porch talking and listening to the night sounds.

Dorie put on the coffee pot and began to calculate when her parents would arrive. It was just about 8:30; she had at least three hours. She would go to the market, clean the bathroom, and make sure that none of his things were lying around. It would be unusual for him to leave anything behind, but there could be a tell-tale pair of underwear or even a condom.

Her parents had met Scriber, and though her father sometimes seemed at a loss for conversation with him, they liked him well enough. She was sure that they would be glad to have her married to a professor. But they did not speak of-ten of it, and they had never mentioned the occasions when Scriber had answered her phone at eleven p.m. or early in the morning. And she had not missed her mother's reaction, during their latest visit, to the blue swimsuit with the strap turned inside out which he had left to dry on the deck railing. Dorie had simply left it there until he came over that afternoon to say hello to her parents and she had said casually that she hoped he had not needed it.

She had seen more of him that first summer than anytime since. When September came, they were both busy, and as the year passed, they had settled down to a routine of a weekly movie and an evening or Sunday afternoon, which seemed ironically like marriage. She had said that to him one Friday evening when they were cooking supper together at his place. He had given her a quick look and then suggested that she should stitch "his" and "hers" on the big white baker's aprons they were wearing.

She had started to say that Todd might not like that— she had dropped in once when he and Scriber were cooking, using a wok to prepare Chinese food—but she had thought better of it. She liked Todd Freeman, if she did feel a little jealous that the graduate student and the professor could talk until well into the night and that there was little else that would keep Scriber up past midnight.

CHAPTER

7

Last summer, Scriber had gone to Europe, alone. After the rigors of finishing his dissertation and getting started in his new job, he welcomed the adventure of exploring some of Europe. He was especially eager to see some of the villages of Germany where Josiah Royce had developed his ideas of the healthful provincialism of small town life. He would set aside a few days for rural Germany.

Dorie had gone with him to New York for a weekend in the city before he flew to London on Sunday night. They took the train, the Southern Crescent, to Washington and then Amtrak's new Metroliner to Penn Station. Before boarding the train to New York, they had lunch at a counter in the cool old station in Washington and walked out to the front, where they could see the Capitol's dome.

The Metroliner was like an airliner, with carpet on the walls, everything quiet as the train slid in and out of the stations. Dorie had fallen asleep after Wilmington; he woke her to look at the Philadelphia skyline and the art museum across the river, pronounced "school-kill." He had lived in this bustling city for a while.

Saturday he showed her the sights that she had read about in the New York City guide book, and they had an early dinner at a crowded little restaurant not far from Lincoln

Center. They had walked across Broadway to see the Chagall murals in the opera house in the fading light that the French call crepuscule—she had taught him the word—and they had sat by the fountain until the curtain rose. The theater, where they saw an Arthur Miller revival, was near a long reflecting pool with trees at one end and a large sculpture in the middle. At intermission they walked around to the other side of the pool and sat on a bench looking back toward the theater with its glass front wall that enabled them to see the people going up and down the red carpeted staircases, and then, all at once, going back to their seats. When she had jumped up, Scriber had said, "Don't hurry."

After the play she had asked him to show her Carnegie Hall. He had looked at her quickly as if surprised. She had not noticed it when they had walked past the old place on their way back to the hotel. Scriber had been very quiet as they walked down 57th Street and seemed not to hear her as she wondered out loud if they could go inside the still lighted hall. Perhaps he had had enough sightseeing, or maybe he is already beginning his looming journey.

On Sunday they had a late breakfast at the hotel and then took a bus down Fifth Avenue to Greenwich Village. She could see the arch long before the bus stopped in front of a large brownstone church with a low iron fence along the sidewalk. She could hear the people singing as she and Scriber turned down the street and stood waiting on the corner for the light. When the light changed, he did not move for a second or two, and she knew that he had been listening to the hymn.

Washington Square was filling with people. The green

benches along the walks were full already, and old ladies and young men with dogs held their own among the young couples with strollers. At the edges of the dry fountain, a dozen or more groups clustered around: folk singers, a West Indian steel band, and a street preacher. Each group was like those pictures you see of the galaxies, tight around the center and trailing off to a tail. She and Scriber had joined the ritual which moved around the fountain, crowding into the knot to see what the singer looked like, trailing off until caught in the gravitational field of the metallic band or the insistent oratory of the black preacher in overalls.

"Yes sir, if Jees' was here, he'd be a farmer. Look a' this town, full o' dirt. We breathe dirt, hear dirt, look at dirt, even eat dirt. Not fit for our chil'ren or for us neither. If Jees' was here, he'd be a farmer in overalls, lovin' the clean earth, seein,' hearin,' breathin,' eatin' clean. I been down to South Carolina, and down there even the dirt is clean. Listen to the Word: 'Whatever is pure, whatsoever is lovely, whatsoever is a good report, think on these things.' Remember Daniel in the king's house, wouldn't eat no fancy food. He jes' lived clean, and he was strong enough for whatever come. This city reminds me of Ninevah, that great city where people din't know their right hand from their left, where God sent Jonah to preach to 'em. And remember how Jeesus stood out there by Jeruzalum, and wept over that city because they was like sheep without no shepherd. Better wear overalls and have a shepherd, and have good clean dirt on your hands than to live with your body and your min' and your heart full of all this dirt."

As they moved away, Scriber said that at least you

could get the theme of his sermon which was more than he could say for many he had heard.

They had walked toward a shaded area to find a place to sit down. Several small boys were tossing a Frisbee, getting in a throw when they could get an opening across the plaza, and sometimes when they couldn't. The missile hit one man, and he kicked the thing and muttered something to the pavement. There were no empty benches, so they had stood, watching people go through the Frisbee's flypath. More often than not the unwary strollers would scowl when the orange saucer came by. A young woman in a blue suit, who looked dressed up enough for any Midwestern Sunday morning, came toward them, her small white hat and the Frisbee on a collision course. She saw it, and with one deft movement caught the Frisbee in a white gloved hand and, in the same movement, sent it with a flick of the wrist and a wide smile to the surprised boy. She dusted her gloves and walked on toward the buff-brick church with the door standing open across the street from the square. "Not all dirt, I guess," Scriber had said, spotting an empty bench and pulling her quickly toward it.

Later, they had gone over to the church to find a water fountain. She waited in the unattended narthex while Scriber went downstairs to the washroom. He came up the stairs proposing a name for the church.

"Let this be called the Church in the Buff of Our Miss Grace of the Orange Frisbee. Do you know that they have real towels and soap down there, and the brass fixtures are polished as if they were expecting company? And I'll bet they get some company in this neighborhood. They've even got a shower stall, for Christ's sake."

Though they didn't get beyond the water fountain and the rest rooms in the basement, it was the first time Scriber and Dorie had been to church together.

Her flight back to the university left JFK airport before his. They had shared an early supper at an old hotel that Scriber said was the place where Thomas Wolfe lived and where someone used to hold a kind of artists' round-table on the radio. The chocolate cake was delicious, and they had time to sit over coffee. It was one of those places where the food came quickly and hot, but you could sit as long as you liked and the waiter would not bring the check until you asked for it.

Scriber talked about his trip: he would be in Paris this time next week. Who would help her keep up the tennis game? He would miss the market and the tomatoes and cantaloupes which were just reaching their peak. What would she like from Europe? (He had, as it turned out, brought her a candle made in Austria with flowers and butterflies carved into it, and she kept it on the buffet and hardly burned it since the first night when they wanted to see what it looked like. He kept saying that there were more where that came from and why didn't she burn it, or was she given to delayed gratification. She did burn it another time, in the bedroom.)

When they arrived at the airport, Scriber kissed her and then said goodbye at the boarding gate. As she walked toward gate 36, she turned and saw him still there. He was wearing a tan suit that he could wash out in a hotel bathroom and wear the next day and a green turtleneck—and he seemed to go up on the balls of his feet when he waved to her. After she had checked in, she walked back to the place where she could see him, but he was gone.

CHAPTER

8

On the plane, Dorie reached up and turned off the light and when the stewardess came by, she told her that, no, she would not be having dinner.

By the time the man on the aisle had finished what looked like blueberry cheesecake, they were halfway to the Graham Regional Airport. Dorie settled back but knew that she would not sleep. She thought about the day, and last night, and imagined Scriber on the plane now, probably getting sleepy, his plane hurtling eastward across the dark Atlantic, Scriber hurrying it along as if he could not get far enough east.

She remembered how he had talked about that once, when they were having breakfast at her place, about traveling east and west and what that meant. On a previous trip to England, he had gone down to Greenwich where the prime meridian runs through a crack in the floor of the observatory, and he had stood there with one foot in the East and one in the West, then on one foot and then on the other to see if he could actually feel the difference. He said that he couldn't, and that it was just green England all the time.

He was telling Dorie about this, sitting on her deck chaise with the paper and café au lait that she had poured from two pots. A plate of Danish sat on the table between them, and the coffee cups were those big white ones that last a long time. The sun was getting a little too high for reading, and she thought he would either put the paper down or ask where his sunglasses were.

"Look at this, Dorie. For the first time since before the War, as many people are moving out of California as are moving in! 'The Bureau of Statistics reported today that the population of the nation's most populous state is stabilizing. Decreased migration to California, and increasing movement out of the state, largely from the Los Angeles area, are probably in large measure due to unemployment in the aerospace industry and to growing concern about the hazards to health of environmental pollution,'" he read. He was excited. "These people are moving back to places like Oklahoma and the Midwest. How about that!"

He gestured with an apricot Danish as he went on. He had once flown out to California for a professors' convention in San Francisco. It was the longest trip west he had taken. He was twenty-eight at the time and going to see, as he put it, "the end of the frontier," for the first time.

"I decided to stop to see my family on the way back rather than on the way out. I wanted to go all the way, from one coast to the other, with no stops between, to be catapulted from East to West, to be three hours younger when I got off the plane than when I got on."

He had laid the paper on his stomach, and he was holding the cup with his fingers folded around it. He seemed to be talking to the geraniums at the end of the redwood deck. "I took the train up to Washington so that I could get a direct flight instead of changing in Atlanta. Washington isn't really on the Atlantic, but you have the feeling of being all the way east that you don't have in Atlanta. The best place to start from would be Boston. But we took off from National Airport and I unfolded the map that was in the pocket and looked for the route. The first thing I saw was that we would enter the Central Time Zone over Kentucky, but decided not to change my watch until we reached San Francisco."

The plane had flown over Oklahoma, and Scriber could see Oklahoma City—he knew it before the pilot said so because of the oil wells around the capitol—and he was able to locate Lincoln from there.

When he had reached San Francisco, he wrote it all down, how he felt looking down on his hometown halfway between the Atlantic and the Pacific. He said he would show it to her some time, but he never did. He had said enough, however, that she knew that it was one of the important things that had happened to him. He was probably more comfortable tonight traveling east, back to the place where the language was born and where the whole western-bent nation had its roots. She closed her eyes and tried to picture him, perhaps having a second dinner even though he would later call it "TV dinner par avion," and then sleeping until they woke him for breakfast. He always fell asleep like an apple falling from a tree and woke up as quickly when the time came.

CHAPTER

9

Dorie carried her peppermint tea—she seldom drank coffee when she was alone—out to the deck. She had put on the jeans she had had since her sophomore year which she had cut off when the knees wore out from too much gardening. Nowadays she would patch them red or yellow, or both, and she did, as a matter of fact, miss having knees when she was digging in the garden or down on the deck tending the plants in red clay pots. One day she was weeding the wildflower garden by the drive—wild iris, birdsfoot violets, Quaker ladies—and Scriber had sat on his bicycle watching her, for five minutes he said, before she saw him.

She put a finger in a pot of geraniums. They didn't need water. This would be a day for geraniums and for Scriber at the beach—warm and sunny.

She was wearing one of his old shirts with the sleeves rolled up and the tail out. That would do for the market. Even the pastel ladies and their quiet men in overalls seemed just as glad for the customers to be as variegated as the vegetables. There was something about the early morning, the comforting bond of having just come from sleeping and dreaming common dreams, wearing their memories on one's face and in the timbre of one's voice that made her comfortable and easy at the market. People didn't expect much of you that early. You had just jumped into your clothes and arrived looking, as nearly as you would ever look again, like a sleepy child. There was no need for small talk. "Good morning," and "I'll have some of those snaps and some little potatoes" was all they expected. But there was more. It wasn't at all like going to Big Star or Winn-Dixie. Here it was cool and by the time the sun had heated the armory's tar roof, the flowers and vegetables would be gone and the pastel women would be home, cooking and canning what they had carried back.

You had to get there early, they said, to get the blackberries and roses before they were sold out, but that suited Dorie who usually went even earlier than this morning, perhaps as much to get there while everyone was still half between waking and sleeping as to get the dewberries before they were gone. She didn't know any place in Collegemont where she could go in cut-offs and Scriber's frayed shirt and feel at the same time close to people and lost in the crowd.

She was late this morning. Scriber would have awakened her earlier. She wondered if he felt the same way about getting there early, or if it was just the blackberries and the smallest zucchini that enticed him. She found what she needed—tomatoes, yellow squash, the last of the blueberries, pole beans and new potatoes, gladiolus, eggs—and then, as usual, she put them in the car and came back to walk up one aisle and down the other just to see if she had missed anything. It was something that she and Scriber did each Saturday, without bothering to ask if the other would like to.

She saw Todd before he saw her, and she knew, when he looked her way, that he was glad to see her but that he didn't want to stop and talk.

"Hi, Dorie," he said as they met by a counter full of potted plants and green apples, first this season, the really sour ones that cook quickly into apple sauce.

"Meet my friend, Gates Sloan. Finding what you want? Where's Scriber?" He didn't know that Scriber had gone to the beach. Dorie was secretly pleased to tell him that Scriber had been wanting some time to get away by himself, and that she was sure it would do him good and what a nice day he had for lying in the sun.

She noticed Gates Sloan looking at her closely. Their conversation had already been long enough to breach the conventions of the market, so she said that she was glad to see them both and that her parents were coming. She had one more aisle to cover and didn't the apples look good. They said goodbye, and as they walked away, it struck Dorie that they seemed to belong together. Todd was taller, but they were both muscular in an aesthetic sort of way, as if they worked out not to build muscles but to keep trim. They both wore jeans that were honestly faded, immaculately laundered, and as close fitting as their shirts.

Todd turned and called to her: "By the way, where did Scrib go?"

She caught the easy masculine familiarity in the diminutive. "Strand Beach. He's never been there and someone told him that it was a kind of old-fashioned place. But they do have a Holiday Inn."

It had slipped out. She hadn't intended to say where Scriber was staying. But then it probably didn't matter.

"Thanks," he said, "we're going to the beach sometime this weekend, but I don't know where. We may go camping."

Gates laughed at that and they said goodbye again. Dorie handed the used paper bag full of apples to the woman in a light blue dress who put them on the hanging scale, adding, "Put in another one or two and make it a good two pounds." Her father liked homemade applesauce.

CHAPTER

10

They arrived just before noon, her mother complaining of the heat and her father explaining that they had not counted on so much traffic on a Saturday morning. "Looks like everyone in creation is going either to the mountains or the beach."

They had seen scores of travel trailers and campers on the road. Her mother had noticed one with chrome letters, "Open Road," and she thought it might be nice to have something like that when Wilbur retired so they could see the country.

"The Masons, you know, go everywhere. She even has a kitchen in there, and a bathroom. I wouldn't mind traveling so much if we had our own bathroom."

"That's right," Dorie said as she handed them some iced tea, "the true religion of America is sanitation. Show a tourist a room looking out on the Alps and he doesn't even see the mountains until he has checked out the good old john. Godliness is next to cleanliness in this country." Her father, who liked to stay home anyway, chuckled, and then asked as he started walking toward it, "Where is the good old john, anyway?"

Dorie knew that lunch would last until 1:30. Her

father would take a nap while she and her mother did the dishes, and then they would go downtown and look in the gift shops where a thousand items from everywhere looked all the same. They would go out for an early dinner at one of the local restaurants that had a contract for a salad dressing and meat sauce, made in some great factory in New Jersey or Chicago, untouched by human hands and formulated especially for college cafes. Her mother would say as they left the restaurant that she had eaten too much and her father would take a toothpick as he paid the bill and slowly explore his teeth as they took a walk through the campus. Later they would sit on the deck for a while and her parents would begin to yawn and then leave her to read or to watch the late movie. Tomorrow they would go to the Presbyterian Church and to the College Inn for Sunday dinner.

Dorie found herself enjoying the predictability of it all. She was much too young to feel that what was going to happen in her life had happened already, but when it came to a weekend with her parents, she knew what to expect—what they were capable of and what she was capable of when she was with them—and she found that she didn't mind. Perhaps that was what home and parents meant, predictability in the face of a changing environment, order amid chaos.

After they had gone to bed, she didn't pick up her book but just sat there in the deep canvas chair and let the night seduce her into slumber.

CHAPTER

11

Scriber lay at an angle to the sea watching the breakers, his head on his arm. When he was younger, his position on the sand had been determined by the position of the sun and by the relative coloration of the various parts of his body. He used to move as predictably as the shadow of a sundial and, at the same time, he would rotate himself systematically like a loin on a spit. And each oscillation and rotation was accompanied by basting with the latest tanning formula from Scandinavia. He could see that younger self occasionally even now on the beach, in the young man with one arm held up like an injured wing, or the woman in the position of a capsized praying mantis.

Today he was letting the sun find him and letting its heat tell him when to turn over or when to go running into the surf with the high step of a man walking on hot sand, catching his breath when the water hit his stomach. The cold water had its own wisdom and would tell him what to do, just as the sun would tell him when to sleep and when to put on his white terry cloth shirt and cover his face with the old tennis hat he had brought along. If he had wanted, he could have relied on the sun to tell him when to eat, just as his farmer uncle once did. He would put his hand over his eyes and look up to see if it was time for Scriber and his cousins to go sit under the tree and eat onion sandwiches or, in the evening, time to stop working and go home to the chores and supper. Today he would eat when he got hungry. He wanted to let it all roll over him, like the sea.

He had a game—some might call it a dance—that he played with the breakers. It was a game that he could play only in the Atlantic. (The Pacific's swells were too big, and he had found the currents at the English beaches too quixotic). But the Atlantic was, in most places, just right. The waves were large enough to lift him, but they were seldom bruising.

As soon as he had come down to the beach, he had gone into the water, running into the surf and diving into the first wave, as he always did. He had seen people stand ankle deep and wet their wrists or put water on their heads before tentatively backing into a hip-deep breaker. He was about swimming as about entering a room full of people: walk in or walk away.

His game was, as a matter of fact, a dance and was more or less the opposite of riding a wave. He stood in the water about navel deep and waited for a swell to begin to lift him. Then he would simply fold his knees and let the wave carry him as it would, toward the shallows and then back toward the deep water. He had learned how to provide a minimum amount of motion by bouncing lightly on the bottom, like a balloon falling on mown grass. He could continue in this movement back and forth, up and down for some time, and the object, if there was an object, was to do as little as possible and to allow the waves to have their way with him.

Once on a beach on the Outer Banks, where the shelf sloped away as gradually as a Kansas road, and where the swells were as long and gentle as the waving of a wheat field, he had gone on for half an hour before he found himself in water so deep that he had to swim back to shore. This morning he had played for at least ten minutes.

He couldn't remember when he had first learned the game. Even in a swimming pool he liked to bounce off the bottom as far as he could go toward the deep end. It was not the sort of game that he could have learned as one would learn water skiing or even swimming. And he wasn't sure that he could teach it to anyone, or that he would even want to try. It had just happened one day when a wave caught him just right, lifted him in the water that was just the right depth to let him bounce and then rise with the next wave. He was not even sure that he knew that it had happened that first time, or even the second. He may have resisted the waves' movement many times before he let himself go and was conscious that he was doing so. But eventually—perhaps he had to be in just the right mood for it—he had felt himself moving easily and following the breakers' lead. Now he could hardly remember being at the beach without playing the game. That was not to say that he came to the beach thinking of the game, or even looking forward to it. But when he was there, it happened.

He did not talk about it, and he was just as glad that people sitting on the beach were preoccupied with each other or with other swimmers. He had hardly ever been conscious of being watched, though once or twice a lifeguard seemed to show him special attention. Once Dorie had watched him when he was not aware that she was not asleep behind her

sunglasses, and she had made some comment about his looking like a bobber on a busy fishing line and had asked just
what was he doing.

"Oh! Just some water calisthenics that I find relax-
ing." She had seemed satisfied with that.

The beach was filling up. A woman with a tall pink
hat that looked like a feather duster put her knitting basket
and her two children down in the spot next to Scriber's. The
children had a beach ball as large as they were which they
began throwing immediately back and forth, catching it with
the exaggerated motions of Atlas lifting the world. Soon tir-
ing of that, they moored the ball in a hanger of sand and went
running and shouting down to the water's edge where they
stopped and jumped up and down, shouting more loudly
than ever.

Scriber could hear the methodical clicking of the woman's knitting needles; he turned to see what she was making.
Whatever it was, it was as pink as her hat, but he was sure
that such a headpiece could not have been knitted. She was
probably making a little jacket for the extra toilet paper in
her bathroom.

He turned his head in the other direction, fell asleep,
and did not wake again until the children, grown hungry,
came running for peanut butter sandwiches, which the woman made on the spot and spread with grape jelly.

Scriber realized that he was hungry, but he did not
move. He enjoyed watching the children eat and then go back
to bouncing the big slow ball that seemed sometimes to stand
still in mid-air.

Suddenly he was very hungry and the sun was hot on

his back. He still did not move, but peeked out from under the tennis hat. He could see one of the children catching and throwing the ball. Beyond was the sea, calm now, the breakers falling gently and running in long sighs to the sand. The very air seemed to pulsate with the heat, and yet was motionless. Scriber himself lay perfectly still and realized that even on the beach he was playing the game. It wasn't that at that moment he began to analyze what the sea symbolized for him, or what the significance of his migration from the country's heartland to the littoral East might mean, or whether going to the beach was some sort of religious experience. Quite the contrary, he just lay there deep in the sand under his tennis hat, like some great turtle shy of people, and registered, without moving, the rhythmical clicking of the knitting needles, the soft bouncing of the ball, the faint cries of the children and the rushing and recession of the sea. He could not have said how long he lay there, or whether he slept again or merely daydreamed. It was the hunger that caused him finally to stir and to make his way slowly, like a man in a daze, back to the motel. He was surprised when he looked at his watch and saw that it was after one o'clock.

Scriber was aware that he felt strange as he dropped his swimsuit on the cold floor. Had he gotten too much sun? Or perhaps he was still half asleep? He caught sight of himself in the mirror and remembered, for some inexplicable reason, Sunday afternoons when he was a small boy in Oklahoma.

There had been about those long afternoons a sterility and loneliness which he had more than once felt subsequently when he walked into a room in which no object had any connection with his life. There had been a silence in his parents' house as the family seemed to pull apart into discreet entities after going to church together and eating what was always a large dinner in the dining room. His mother often sat reading in the big chair by the front window, and his father took a long nap in their room upstairs. Sometimes their relations came by, but they knew to come toward suppertime when his father had come back downstairs and his mother had put her magazine down and gone into the kitchen to set out the cold food.

The children had to be quiet and were not allowed to leave the yard on Sunday. On those afternoons Scriber had read the funny papers slowly (glad now for his friends who did not observe the Sabbath too closely. Last Christmas one of Scriber's ecology-minded friends had given him a gift wrapped in the Sunday comics. As he had opened the package, he had felt something that had little to do with what was inside, a bittersweet ambivalence for those Sunday afternoons in Lincoln with his father asleep upstairs and his mother reading in the front room and everything feeling different from other days).

The tiles were cold under his feet. The bathroom seemed pristine, never used by another human being. He had started staying at these places because they were predictable: the bathrooms were always clean and the food was what you would expect from a motel that prided itself on catering to the traveling family—decently palatable. This place was no exception. The glasses were wrapped in plastic, fresh towels were lined up like valets, and despite all the swimmers who had come carelessly through here, he was sure that no grain of sand lingered. It was as if the entire bathroom were flushed down the toilet after each occupant's departure and the whole thing built anew. He had traveled in Europe enough to appreciate these gleaming comforts. At the same time, he remembered that he had used, as a boy, the two-holer at his uncle's farm where the signs of human use were unmistakable and unavoidable, even on Sunday. The last word he would use to describe that experience was sterility. But that was what he was feeling now, sterility, as he stood there testing the water so he could wash off the salt and sand from his morning by the sea.

He would just get into his old jeans and go for a quick lunch in the restaurant, unimpressive as it was. The pseudo-rustic cafe was one of the two places where the motel resembled an inn, a place for travelers to be together, as in a common room. The other was the swimming pool, though even there people succeeded in isolating themselves from the people with whom they shared the sterilized water. For the most part motels, especially those without bars, were much like those suburbs without sidewalks, without places for meeting people in the normal routine of shared life.

CHAPTER

12

A dozen or more people were having a late lunch, about half of them alone. It was a pattern. Half of the cars on the way down had carried only one passenger, and now Scriber sat down at a table set for four to have lunch a few feet from several other people also dining with three empty chairs. He would have been the first to complain if the inn were to go "family style," but he did wonder if there might be some hidden benefits associated with living in a less affluent society which could ill afford the isolation of the private table, the private automobile, the private room for every member of a family. But he had, after all, decided to come to the beach alone, and he wasn't at all sure that he wished to talk with anyone, any more than he welcomed the sight of a casual acquaintance when boarding a plane. About this, as about many things, he felt a painful ambivalence, uncomfortable with the distance he felt but not sure that he had the stomach for the enforced intimacy of another era. For the moment, he wanted to eat and get back to the beach.

The waitress, like the girl at the desk and the boy at the pool, was obviously a college student or perhaps even in high school. He wondered if students could spot a professor as easily as he identified undergraduates. He had been in the stacks of the Library of Congress one day when a young girl had said, "After you, Professor," as she backed down the one-way staircase to let him pass. He had not been thirty at the time, and it had jolted him, like the first time a graduate student had called him "sir."

The young woman stood waiting with pad and pencil. When he looked up from the menu he saw that she had been looking intently at him.

"I'll have deviled crabs and a salad with oil and vinegar, and some iced tea."

When she repeated the order, he knew by the way she said "oil" that she was from the South, but her speech showed education as well. She was wearing a starched calico dress and there was about her that close-to-the-earth look that he saw in Dorie. She had dark hair under a stiff little cap that matched the dress, and a full round face that would one day have a double chin if she were to become a farmer's wife. As she walked to the kitchen, she was still writing on the pad and showing it the same intent attention she had paid him when she thought he was not looking.

When she came to the table the third time, to ask if he would like dessert, he asked her what people did at Strand Beach in the evening. She looked surprised. Then she blushed, so slightly that in anyone with a complexion less clear it would have gone unnoticed. It had been a long time since he had seen anyone blush, and when he had last blushed he could not recall, though he now remembered that it had happened often when he was a teenager. He started to say something further, just to relieve her of the need to speak.

But before he could say anything, she said with unexpected composure, "Well, my friends and I go to Sea Camp on Saturday night to practice for Sunday. We're in the choir."

He had noticed the name on a road sign earlier. "Sea Camp? Where is that?"

"Oh, just across that inlet that they call Sunday Lake. It's not really a lake, and it's not named for the day either but for Billy Sunday who preached in the auditorium. There is a big church that they call the tabernacle. People come from everywhere, and many of them stay in those little canvas houses that cluster close to the tabernacle. People stay for a week or even a month, to hear the preachers who come from all over, and the hymn singing is great. The Methodists opened Sea Camp as a beach-front camp meeting in the last century. It makes for quite a contrast, next door to the Strand."

She would have gone on, but he interrupted.

"Do you live around her?"

"No," she said, "I'm from Avery, but this is the second summer Mark and I have come to the Camp. He takes care of maintenance here at the inn, and we live at the Cedars."

She seemed to feel free to talk now, though she was looking around to see if the remaining customers might be signaling for more iced tea or a check.

"The Cedars?"

"Oh, it's a boarding house, actually. Cedars of Lebanon. You just follow the boardwalk past the Ferris wheel and when you get to the old houses, it's the fifth one, not far from the auditorium."

A man across the room raised one finger as if he were testing the wind, and she took her pad out of a pocket and began walking toward him, but not before she smiled at Scriber and said, "Have a nice day, and do walk over to the Camp."

He sat for a while, moving the ice around the bottom of his glass. He still didn't know what people did on Saturday night in these very different twin towns.

For just about as long as he could remember, certainly for all of his adult life, Scriber had taken a nap after lunch. There were, of course, days when it was not possible, and once he had been deprived of his siesta twice a week for a whole semester by an early afternoon seminar. But even then, right after lunch, he had stretched out on the floor of his office with the door locked, hoping that the phone would not ring.

He had learned from one of his teachers, Dr. Howard, that a nap after lunch made the evening more productive, so he could, in the good conscience of a son of the Protestant work ethic, regard his nap as an investment. Old Dr. Howard, his graduate professor, had suggested he sleep no longer than thirty minutes—"Better too little than too much,"—he had said. (He had applied Professor Howard's advice to his dutiful style of life as well.)

Scriber's regimen was to lie down in his office with a pencil in one hand dangling over the side of the couch. When the pencil hit the floor, it was time to wake up.

Today he would alter his routine by sleeping on the beach but he had no intention of working either before or after dinner.

CHAPTER

13

The sand was hot on his feet so he did a kind of running dance to the place which was still marked by the tall pink hat and striped beach ball. The children were sleeping under the umbrella, and their mother, who had put her needles down, was sitting at the edge of the shade, propped against a fold-up beach chair. He could not tell whether she was asleep or contemplating the orange peelings between her legs.

There were more people on the beach than earlier, but they seemed to add to the general somnolence. A few children played at the water's edge, and a lone swimmer, out beyond the breakers, bobbed up and then disappeared with each wave. A young woman of marriageable age and more than marriageable proportions occupied an Indian blanket not far from Scriber's spot. Her head was on one arm and the other arm was thrown across the blanket as if to reserve that space for someone.

Scriber, still wearing his swimsuit, shirt, and hat, stretched out on his beach towel, its great orange butterflies swarming on a field of purple. Dorie had given him the towel for his last birthday. He had come back from a trip to San Francisco just in time for the party. She had baked a cake and invited some people over. When he had opened the package and held the towel up to himself like a woman sizing up a dress in the mirror, someone had said, "Anyone got a net?" And several eyes had turned toward Dorie. But she either missed it or refused to acknowledge the remark, and had gone on merrily handing him packages and asking if anyone would like more cake.

They had all shown great interest in his trip to San Francisco, Todd especially, and he had talked at length about places to eat and what to do in North Beach and yes, he had been to one of the topless places. He did not mention that he had gone to church with one of his colleagues. No one had asked him about that.

He had stayed late at Dorie's after everyone else had gone home. He had helped her wash up and then they sat out on the deck. He had felt at home.

"You like the towel? I know it's a little wild. Maybe you would like a tiger or something like that better. We could exchange it." She was not really worried that he did not like it. It was just conversation.

"Sure I like it. Butterflies are, after all, ancient symbols for new life. Anyone who likes D.H. Lawrence as much as I do should be happy on a bed of psychedelic butterflies, come to think of it."

He wasn't sure she had read D.H. Lawrence but she seemed satisfied. "Well, I'm glad. Did you really have a good trip? I know how you feel about California, that it is some kind of giant slug, creeping over the whole country and leaving a coat of plastic and asphalt wherever it goes."

That was when he had told her about the experience in the plane thirty thousand feet over Oklahoma. It was the first time he had flown over his home state on his way west. Usually he would land at Oklahoma City and his parents and younger sister would meet him at the gate. But he had decided, on this trip, to spend extra time in San Francisco and then to fly directly back East.

The Mississippi had looked like a wide highway. The boats and barges, which he could see easily, made for considerable traffic, and the river was intersected like any major road by the two-stream interstates. Where there should have been clover leaves, there were bridges to separate the traffic that rolled from that which swam.

Then there was Arkansas. He knew there were hills and even mountains down there. His grandparents had taken him one summer to visit a farm up in the northwest corner of the state, the White River country. They had driven very slowly in his grandfather's old black Chevrolet with seats that were woolly like the big chairs in his grandmother's front room. And he remembered, too, that the woman's name was Aunt Bertie. Her family grew peach trees and she made something from peaches for just about every meal: cobbler, pie, upside-down cake, pancakes, ice cream in a hand-turned churn. From up here he couldn't see anything of this state but green trees. Even where the mountains should have been, it looked only a little bumpy.

But he knew when they had reached Oklahoma. The land began to flatten out and the trees grew lonely and grouped themselves in copses and in long lines along the creeks. He knew that most of them were blackjack oaks and that they would not be as brightly green for the rest of the summer as they were now.

Lots of them surrounded the farmhouse where he had been born with the help of a doctor who had managed to wait for him by joining the baby's grandfather in getting a little drunk on the sheriff's confiscated whiskey as they received the news from England that Edward VIII had renounced the throne. For his trouble Dr. Scriber Robinson had been given fifty dollars and had the red squalling thing named after him.

Scriber always went, on his visits home, to the office with his first name on a brass plate, across from the courthouse. Once, just after he had graduated from college and been written up in the local paper because his aunt knew the woman who wrote such columns, the old doctor had asked, pretending that his memory had failed him, "Who taught who, Plato or Socrates?"

The old man had always shown a keen interest in the flesh which bore his name and Scriber, too, upon arriving at home would ask before he had been there long, "How is the doctor?" He always got the same answer: the old man was still making house calls and still had "his problem."

He had spotted the town of Lincoln easily. The Sandy River's banks and mud flats were a distinct red line to the south. That meant that Lincoln was just to the left of the plane. He waited, and then he saw the water tower that looked like a steel top hat on four legs. Next appeared the sandstone courthouse where his grandfather's office had been, with its four-sided clock tower and its surrounding green lawn and large oak trees and he knew that he was looking at the street paved with red bricks where he had lived as a boy after they moved to town.

The plane then hovered for a second, directly over his

grandparents' farm, and though the room in which he had been born was now the new tenant's dining room, he felt suddenly like a salmon, or one of those fantastic eels, or a strong-winged bird, nearing its spawning place. He held his breath, sure that the plane was going to turn nose down, like the water witches that people in Oklahoma carved out of willows and declared would take a nose dive when good water was near. He was gripping the seat handles, and he began to sweat.

When he looked out the window again, Lincoln had disappeared from view. He had felt simultaneously weak and exhilarated, and when the stewardess suddenly appeared and asked him to put down his table for the tray she held over his head, he had found himself very hungry.

He had told Dorie about it that night after the birthday party in a tone that revealed his surprise at the whole experience. He had never once felt homesick for Lincoln, and yearly visits to his family, while not unpleasant, were often undertaken more out of duty than either pleasure or need. He had, on a few occasions, been joshed by Easterners about being from the wilds of Oklahoma, but he had not felt the need either to stick up for the place or to conceal his origins. He had always had positive feelings about his hometown, or at worst, neutral associations.

He had grown up on a nice street near the Presbyterian Church, and his family's name, Newall, was as respected as it was common in the county. His mother changed all the linen in the house every Monday, and even his homemade school shirts were starched and ironed by hand. His grandfather had bought the first "Victrola" in the county, and they always had a car that was clean and smooth-running when it was time for a drive on Sunday afternoon.

He had seen his grandfather's name and face, above the word "Sheriff," tacked up along roadsides and in store windows during most of his boyhood. He could not deny that he found some pleasure in walking down Main Street and being recognized as the hometown boy become professor. But he had been surprised by what he had felt six miles above the place.

"You didn't expect it, did you?" Dorie had not taken long to see that he was puzzling over it, trying to understand what it meant. He didn't turn to look at her, but he knew she was watching him.

He spoke to the darkness beyond the pots of geraniums.

"I guess I thought that was pretty far away, farther in time even than in space. Do you put stock in the idea that blood is thicker than water, whatever that means?" He didn't give her time to answer. "It was as if my body, quite apart from what I had thought about my hometown and the Baptist Church and the people there, sensed home and was pulled toward the place. Do you know, Dorie, I had to ask the guy next to me to stand up with his tray so that I could squirm my way out from under my own lunch, hungry as I was, to go to the rest room and throw up. And then I ate everything they had and fell asleep like a baby. I didn't wake up until the pilot came on the overhead speaker to point out Lake Tahoe and Donner Pass, where all those people going West had died in a blizzard. And to tell the truth I hardly thought about Lincoln for the five days I was out there, except to send the folks some post cards.

"On the way back we flew not too far to the north of the spot, so that if I had used my imagination, I could have seen our county down there where the land turned green. But it wasn't the same. I wonder if that experience could happen again, or if it could ever happen if I was someday just thinking about it."

They had sat up late, Dorie listening as he talked about how Lincoln was halfway between West and East, and how he felt about each, and what was one to do with the past and a place like Lincoln today. California seemed all new, and the East seemed to be moving that way. He was tired of change, but did that mean that he wanted to get back to Lincoln? Maybe, he had mused out loud, the trauma above Oklahoma was an extreme manifestation of an ambivalent homesickness that seemed to run through the whole country these days. What was newness, and how did it relate to the old, to his living here in a place where he had no blood kin, jetting out to the fabulous West, and in the process, getting half sick in a plane that had no sooner cast a shadow on his birthplace than it was gone.

Dorie had sat smiling, just barely most of the time, more to herself than at him. But he had the feeling she understood when he said that to this day he somehow connected newness with the fresh old sheets that his mother always put on the bed, and with the pillowcases that his grandmother had embroidered with little flowers and the letter "N." Actually, those pillowcases had worn out and his mother had cut off the embroidery and sewn it on to new linen. And he was sure that if he were there now, those pillows would still be on the bed in his room, as old as his memory and as the blood from which it seemed he could not separate himself, and as fresh as his mother's fastidiousness could make them.

Dorie interrupted him. "Isn't what you call newness just a way of being together? Only people make me feel new inside, and what is wrong with the old and the new is that they get in the way of our being people here and now, and with the important people in our past—family, friends, teachers, our buddies—for that matter."

She paused, and then went on. "I don't know what that has to do with your doing a flip over Lincoln, Oklahoma, but it seems to make sense in my own case. Take my parents, for example. They were so hung up on the way it used to be, which they had turned into the way it ought to be—as if the way it used to be was ever that way at all—that they couldn't see me for a long time. They had my life all cut out on a pattern inherited from the family and the church, or whatever. And I was so determined to cut the apron strings and strike out that I couldn't see them, what really decent people they are, even human people who sleep together the night before they go off to church like good Presbyterians. Funny, isn't it, the little girl that they try to make fit their proper pattern is here because they have sex, or did once. When it comes down to it, I'll bet that it is the blood that matters.

"Anyway, we have made life better for one other by trying to see each other. And there is a kind of newness in that. I don't think we would even have tried if there weren't something to that notion of blood being thicker than water. Our relationship, don't you think, Scriber, has about it some of the elements of a caring family, and we have worked in our own way to make it even more so."

He had been in too philosophical a mood to talk about anything as specific as Dorie's parents. He suggested a walk, and when they got back, it was time to go to bed. When he woke up the next morning, he knew that he and Dorie were closer than before.

CHAPTER

14

Scriber had allowed these thoughts to run through his mind many times, and as he lay on the beach it occurred to him that he was by the sea alone as a result of the persistence of the questions he had raised with Dorie that night. He was letting the experience and their conversation take place again in his mind, which lay as quietly as his body, which by now had molded the sand to his contours.

He suddenly felt something like cold rain on his back and arched himself up quickly to see Todd standing over him, quite wet, in a red, white, and blue bikini like those he had seen on the televised Olympics.

"Hi, Scrib. You looked like everyone else under that hat, but I would know your butterflies anywhere. This is my friend, Gates Sloan. OK if we join you?"

He began to sit down when Scriber, moving to get up, said: "I've been lying here in the sun too long. How about going into the water a bit?"

Todd looked at his friend, who said, "Fine with me," and then began stripping off his tank top to reveal a slight but well-proportioned frame. Scriber noticed at once that he wore a small gold cross on a chain around his neck. If he played Scribner's game in the waves, he would lose that for sure. As it turned out, Gates stood in the water no more than knee deep and occasionally splashed water on his face, taking care, it seemed to Scriber, not to get water on his hair, which was very dark and well groomed.

But Todd went with him under the first wave, and they swam out to ride the swells. They had been swimming together before, and he had even tried to teach Todd about the game, but with little success. Todd was the sort who swam laps at the college pool. At the beach he was likely to swim up and down, parallel to the shore, as if he were swimming in marked lanes. One could see in his physique the same discipline that Scriber knew characterized him as a student. And so today, after they had paddled up and down a few times, and Todd had shouted that Dorie had said he might be up here, Scriber moved closer to shore and Todd began to crawl up and down in the troughs, his head low in the water and his stroke as steady as if he were in the smooth water of the college pool working out with the team. By now Gates was sitting on the beach, his arms locked around his knees, surveying the scene through large sunglasses.

Todd had come out of the water without stopping or speaking and had gone jogging down the beach. Scriber shook out his towel and spread it closer to where Gates was sitting. He sprawled out to get all the available sun as the afternoon began to turn toward evening. Neither spoke for a long time. The younger man seemed to be content just to watch the passing show, or perhaps, either out of shyness or in deference to the distance between student and professor, he was waiting for the older man to speak. Scriber perceived this as mild embarrassment. Perhaps he had communicated in some subtle way that he was not entirely happy that Todd had spotted him under his turtle-shell hat on the field of betraying butterflies.

He asked the usual questions. Gates was studying art history and was interested in American painting, especially the New York school of abstract painters. He was from a small town near the border of North Carolina and Virginia, and he hoped to become either a painter or a teacher. Failing that, he would open an art shop in some interesting place like Washington or Atlanta. It was clear that, once started, he enjoyed talking about himself, and at times, usually when he spoke of what he wanted to do in the future, he grew animated and used his supple hands expressively. Scriber found himself wishing the boy would take off his sunglasses, which obscured half his face, though in doing so their dark lenses served to call even more attention to his fine white teeth.

Gates made a wide gesture as he spoke to the surf:

"I would like to have a big old house, one with really good stuff in it, so that I could fix it up. I like those old townhouses they have in Washington. The trouble with going to Atlanta is that there wouldn't be many really old houses to choose from. But I wouldn't mind a nice old Victorian either. All that gingerbread and the pointy roofs and even the stained glass can be beautiful. There are some good ones in that camp place down the beach where the old folks and Jesus freaks hang out."

He had a way of talking which seemed to require no response. Scriber found that he could listen to the young man and the surf at the same time, and in much the same way. That was not to say that Gates was uninteresting. It was just that he was perfectly capable of carrying on a conversation without foil or adversary. Talking with him was more like overhearing someone talking with himself. Scriber wasn't sure that it was nerves that drove his behavior. He might have been able to say had he been able to see the boy's face. But the young man looked at the surf as he talked, turning his head only occasionally to watch someone walk down the beach, or to look in the direction in which Todd had disappeared. And when he did turn toward Scriber, the glasses hid his expression.

When Todd returned, Scriber was stretched out on his back with the tennis hat pulled over his eyes, relaxed as a trusting puppy, its stomach available for fondling. Gates was looking at the sea and talking about old houses and how they were superior to the ones being built now.

"Sure," Todd said as he sat down beside Scriber, seeming not at all winded, "those old places are more interesting than Everyman's split level. I can get good vibrations out of woodwork that has as many coats of paint as it has seen generations. But who has time to be steaming and scraping old wallpaper and painting gables? Unless you like that sort of thing, of course. I'd rather play tennis."

"To each his own," Gates answered. Scriber saw him exchange a long smile with Todd, and he had the strong impression that he was supposed to understand its meaning.

"By the way, Scrib," Todd added, "it's been two weeks since we played."

CHAPTER

15

A fter they had gone, having promised to meet them for dinner, Scriber walked down the beach in the direction of the amusement park. The sun was moving to his right, more warm than hot now, and on his left the sea turned a darker blue. Few children were on the beach at this hour, and he noticed the gulls for the first time today, some of them as raucous as crows and others sailing over the water with a precision that mirrored silence. He passed the Ferris wheel and then walked under a pier. The pilings actually supported a large pavilion decorated with copper dolphins and sailing ships, turned milky green by time and the salt air.

He could hear the music of a carousel despite the amplified sound of the surf as it broke among the pilings. Mixed with the smell of the sea were the faint sweet odors of a carnival. He stood still in the cool shadows, listening, until a large wave that had broken beyond the end of the pavilion came twisting and surging among the mussel-laden pillars to lick his feet with its cold tongue.

He was surprised to see, as he emerged onto the beach, that on each piling were a chain and hook; the beach could be closed to pedestrians, just as red velvet ropes announced that the boxes of a theater were off-limits.

Just beyond was a sign, neatly lettered in modified Gothic script:

SEA CAMP MEETING ASSOCIATION
NO SWIMMING ON SUNDAY
SUITABLE ATTIRE REQUIRED
WELCOME

This part of the beach was beautiful, stretching in a long curve to the fishing pier a mile or more away. Few people were on the sand, and only one couple that he could see were in the water, as if the blue law was in effect already.

He tried to figure out what it was, this sudden stillness that he now felt in the dark underbelly of the carnival. The boardwalk, which passed his motel, made its way across the pavilion above, its sounds muffled. People sat in quiet pairs on benches, facing the sea, the sun behind them. Scriber could not see their faces or the colors of their clothing.

He could still hear the distant sound of the carousel, but quiet reigned here, captured in the receding tide and the way the motionless pairs sat likes doves on the telephone wires along an Oklahoma road.

But it was what lay west of the boardwalk that fascinated him. Perhaps it was merely the contrast to the Strand's roller coaster and electric cars. The street along the beach was entirely without neon lights, not a candy store or soda fountain to be seen. All the houses were relics of the turn of the century, with turrets and towers and high gables, all silhouetted now against the coming sunset. Every house had a long porch, most adorned by large urns of flowers. He was sure that they would be red geraniums.

He walked slowly, trying to remember. Was it Brighton Beach where the houses were old and where King George had built a pavilion and thus helped to preserve the town from the ravages of commercialism? Long stretches of waterfront like this faced the sea at Brighton and lined up along either side of the narrow parks that ran for two or three blocks perpendicular to the beach. He had gone down there once for a weekend out of London, on a beautiful old train with wicker seats, "The Brighton Belle." But even Brighton had some new buildings along the waterfront, and you could locate the cafes and chemists from the beach.

But this place, Sea Camp, seemed, thus far, utterly consistent with its Victorian beginnings. He would not have been surprised had there been no electric lights in the houses. Rather, the residents would sit around Aladdin lamps or just spend the evening out on the porch in the dark, the way his grandparents did in the summer.

He was thinking that he should turn back to dress for dinner when he saw it. A quarter of a mile back from the beach, at the head of one of those long parks such as the one on which his hotel in Brighton had stood, a large white neon cross was shining steadily. He could not make out the structure on which it stood, but it was as tall as a lighthouse, easily the highest structure in the town of lofty Victorian roofs. He stood with his back to the sea and watched the sun go down as the lights began to come on in the houses that faced each other across the park. He was glad that the Sea Camp Meeting Association had not put something like "Jesus Saves" up there, given the commercial advertising which they had banned from the rest of the town. The only neon in town was a cross, which seemed to loom larger and larger as he turned and walked back toward the Strand.

On another occasion, or had he been with someone, he might have expressed the same sort of offense he had taken at the church near his parents' home which played recorded church music for everyone within a mile, whether they wanted it at nine o'clock on Sunday morning or not. As he turned away, it was not a quick turning on his heel, rather he headed back to the hotel slowly, wanting to know more and already promising himself he would return.

The chains were up already, guarding the beach against Sabbath-breaking. He ducked under and walked quickly through the darkness toward the dancing lights and the monotonous music of the carousel. The sea was quiet now, its sound drowned out by the carnival. A fresh breeze blew toward the shore, and beneath his feet the sand felt cold like the tiles of a basement lavatory.

CHAPTER

16

Todd and Gates were late. He had walked through the restaurant looking for them and then gone back outside. The bench on the boardwalk had a movable back, like the seats in the old Erie-Lackawanna commuter train that he used to ride from New York to visit a friend in New Jersey. He moved the seat back to its people-watching position and sat down, first to admire the soft shine on his brown loafers—he hadn't really wanted that gold buckle—and then to watch the passing parade. He was, however, soon absorbed not in watching the people strolling past but in the conversation going on just beside him, on the next bench.

A young couple sat facing the beach. The man was not over twenty and the women looked even younger. A boy who looked younger still leaned against the iron railing, and a boy probably the same age sat next to the young woman. This lad had turned intently toward the couple, holding an open book on one patched knee. All of them were well-scrubbed and looked healthfully robust. The younger boys had longer hair, shining clean, and their clothes looked like they had been worn daily, washed weekly, and patched at every strategic point over the past five years. The largest patches were on the knees, and Scriber wondered if the back pockets had been repaired as extensively. (He had noticed that his students wore their most remarkable patches au derriere or in the fig-leaf regions. Perhaps a whole new art form would emerge alongside phrenology, palmistry, and astrology—patch reading.)

"I was bisexual before I became a Christian," the boy leaning on the rail was saying. The nametag pinned to his chest read "New Life Church—Steve."

"Jesus took all that away, just like that. It's just like the Bible says, 'Except a man be born again, he cannot see the kingdom of God. John 3:3.' "

The couple sat very still and neither spoke. The boy with the Bible—"New Life Church—Tim," had been turning pages. He put his finger on a place and read: " 'That which is born of the flesh is flesh; and that which is born of the spirit is spirit. Marvel not that I said unto thee, ye must be born again.' John 3: 6-7."

The two young evangelists, Steve and his apprentice, Tim, seemed to be waiting for some response. The fellow sitting on the bench with his girl, sensing that, asked with a quickness which was either anxiety or impatience: "Are you guys what they call 'Jesus freaks'? I saw in the paper the other day that some of those 'born agains' punched a gay guy right here on this beach."

The pair looked at each other, and then the one with the Bible spoke. "Some people call us freaks, just like the Bible said: 'We are fools for Christ's sake,' 1 Corinthians 4:10. If that's what you mean by 'freak,' then OK, I'm glad to be a freak for Jesus. It's better than being freaked out over drugs or sex or harassing people."

Steve, still standing up, had glanced over at Scriber,

and the way he spoke suggested that he intended to be overheard.

"The guy that got pushed around was making a pass at people right down there under the boardwalk. Somebody else might have really roughed him up. The people that did it probably did him a favor by getting him off the beach."

"You mean you think the way to help people might be to beat them up?"

It was the woman, who had become suddenly animated as she turned to the boy with the Bible.

"What does that have to do with Jesus, for Christ's sake? What would you hit him with, a cross, or maybe one of those big black bibles you carry around?"

"We didn't hit him with anything," Tim said. "And I'm not saying it was a good thing."

As he spoke, he closed the Bible and laid it on the bench. He had sensed that he and his partner had become defensive, which, for an evangelist, was no ground at all. Steve joined in. "Look, that guy has his problems, and you have yours. How about you, have you been born again?"

The girl had not said her whole piece.

"Born again? Beating people up to save them sounds like the Defense Department, or like hammering out nice little robots. What has that to do with anything remotely resembling human birth, or rebirth, for that matter?" She paused. "I've been to Sunday school. Isn't there something about the Spirit being like the wind? You can't see it or get your hands on it, but it's there, like the wind."

The boy reached toward the Bible, then thought better of it.

His partner said, in a tone which suggested that they were going to move on, "Our church is at Second and Lake, tomorrow at 10:30 and 7:00."

"Is that the one with the big cross on it?" her companion asked.

"No," said Steve, "that's the Tabernacle across the lake in the Camp. Mostly old people go there. Ours is in Strand Beach, just two blocks back from the fun zone. 10:30 and 7:00 tomorrow."

Tim picked up his Bible and stood up, holding the book as a Victorian lady would hold her fan while talking. But before they could get away, the young man who was still seated, rather slouchily, asked in an off-hand tone, looking directly at the boy standing in front of him:

"By the way, are 'bisexual' and 'Christian' mutually exclusive terms? You said you were one and now you are the other."

The boy, arrested in flight, leaned back on the rail, but not easily. He put one foot behind as if to brace himself.

"What I mean is that Jesus took the place of all that. I was living for sex, and taking it wherever I could find it. Now, I'm living for Jesus, and I don't even want the other."

"You mean," the young man asked in a steady voice— the girl was looking out to sea—"that you have given up sex, that that's being born again?"

The boy answered quickly. "Yes, I just couldn't handle it. And now I have something better." He looked at his partner and made it clear that they were leaving.

"God bless you," he said, and they were gone.

As the two walked down the boardwalk, Scriber heard

the young man say to the girl, "I sure hope there is some-place between not being able to handle it and giving it all up for Jesus."

She didn't answer but moved closer to him as he took her hand.

CHAPTER

17

Scriber saw Todd and Gates before they saw him. Todd, always elegantly underdressed, was wearing jeans that looked tailored and a blue and white checkerboard shirt with a large open collar. He looked every inch a tennis player and even now moved with the easy angularity of an athlete, his step even lighter in deck shoes.

Gates looked equally smart, in closely cut linen trousers the color of cream—the buttons were on the outside—and a kind of see-through brown shirt with the top three buttons open. He walked mincingly, and his glance darted around as if he were looking for someone among the oncoming pedestrians.

Scriber watched them, noticing that they were not speaking to each other. He got up to meet them as they approached the door of the beachfront restaurant, "The Galley." Gates saw him and smiled quickly. Both Gates and Todd had the slightly dazed look of someone who has had a long nap in the afternoon and cannot quite shake it off.

Gates seemed still to be looking for someone as they entered the restaurant. Most of the customers were young and, it seemed at first glance, male. When the food came, it was clear to Scriber that the management relied for attracting a clientele on the nautical decor and a kind of dark intimacy rather than on a good kitchen. But Scriber found the place interesting, though he would have been at a loss to answer in specific terms the question which had been in Todd's eyes since they had sat down: 'What do you think of the place?' Had he tried to answer the unspoken thought, he would have remarked that it seemed ironic that there should be so little light in a room with so many mirrors, and in which a good many of the customers shared in Gates' rubbernecking preoccupation.

The young man was even now looking not at Todd or Scriber, who were poorly lit by the leaded-glass version of a ship's lantern suspended over their table, but was taking inventory of the eight or nine tables in the room, like a quarterback talking to his team while sizing up the opposition. Scriber found the habit distracting, even irritating. What was more, he noted the same curious glances in his direction from more than one young man in the room. He began to feel like an outsider, as if most of the people here had something in common which he did not share, and by some cabalistic sign among themselves, or by some signal which he was unconsciously emitting, he had been identified as the exotic in their midst. It wasn't that people stared at one another or at him. It was rather a covert solicitousness, a quick darting of the eyes or a long sideward glance as, for example, that coming from a young man who pulled hard on a cigarette and then stabbed it half a dozen times into the ash tray.

The mirrors, Scriber realized, were useful in this regard. It was possible to look directly at almost any person in the room without appearing to do so. It occurred to him that

that was precisely what a conversation with Gates felt like: talking with him was like speaking to someone who looked at a mirror behind one's head in which he could keep in touch with everything going on around him and, at the same time, carry on a lively dialogue with minimal engagement. It was like talking with half a person. Not that the conversation was not witty or entertaining; far from it. Anonymous or perfunctory sex must be like this, fun but fundamentally impersonal. Gates' conversation struck him as talk for the sake of talk, little more. Perhaps one should not expect more than that at cocktail parties or during a first evening out with a friend's friend at a place with strobe lights on mirrored walls to simulate the undulations of the sea.

Todd, by contrast, appeared to be above it all. He clearly knew several people in the restaurant, including the undergraduate waiter in blue jeans and tank top. He spoke to the young man with a familiarity that was also affectionate. But Todd, unlike Gates, was present. As Gates became increasingly absent, the conversation fell to the older pair.

The three of them had stopped on the way in at a table of four men. To be sure, it is always awkward to stand up looking down at people trying to eat dinner. But it had struck Scriber as curious that all of the introductions had been by first name only. What was even stranger was the unmistakable way in which Todd had singled him out by the tone of his voice: "This is my tennis partner, Scrib. We just happened to meet on the beach today. He's never been here before."

Once at their table, Scriber said, in the detached seriousness of one reminiscing: "We used to go to a place in New York, near Columbia. They had the same kind of mock-

Tiffany lights. A German friend of mine taught me the word kitsch in that place. 'The Brass Ring' they called it, and a finer example of kitsch I haven't found. But somehow at night after studying hard, it was just the place. The library would empty out into the restaurant. Even the food matched the atmosphere, mostly overloaded sandwiches and sticky desserts, but they served good homemade soup.

"I remember, there was a little old lady, very old, who was there every night. She had her own table, just a little larger than a bar stool, right in the middle of the place. I never saw her talk to anyone. She just sat there drinking what looked like iced tea, watching all those young people come and go as if she were a house mother who had given up giving advice or keeping discipline. She always wore the same blue dress, the color of old crepe paper, and a little round hat with some kind of net around it. She would look straight at you without communicating anything at all, neither an invitation to speak to her, nor pity, nor condescension. Nothing. She would just look at you and sit there and drink the same drink all evening. I decided that she probably lived in a threadbare little room around there somewhere and that The Brass Ring was the only place where she could get away from her fussy landlady with her unpleasant Chihuahua, or that room, or whatever. The place was always well-heated, too, in winter, and she may have been there for sheer animal warmth. I wasn't there in the summer time, and I've wondered if she sat out on the shady benches along Broadway, or if she spent her summer evenings in The Brass Ring. Nobody knew her name. We asked several waiters about that."

Scriber was sure that Gates had heard all of this, but

he did not respond.

"I don't think I have seen any old people in here," Todd said. "Most of them are happier over at the Camp."

Gates was looking alternately at his plate and at the mirror behind Todd. Todd continued: "You can see them, mostly old couples who hold hands walking at night in the Strand. They walk for a mile or more up the boardwalk, just looking at everyone and enjoying the bright lights and the candy shops. They have the same need for a little action that makes your bar in New York a hangout for students, or, on the other hand, that sends swingers to church. The traffic goes two ways between the Strand and the Camp, though these days it seems that the Strand gets the lion's share."

"What is the Camp?" Scriber asked. "I think I saw it, or at least part of it, today when I was down the beach beyond that big pavilion."

Todd hesitated, looking at Gates. "Well, I don't know much about it, except that they have a big tabernacle over there—you can see it from this side of the lake—and people come and stay, some of them all summer. There are lots of big old turn-of-the-century places, mostly boarding houses, and some people rent places right around the Tabernacle.

As a matter of fact, I went there a couple of times with my folks—we were Methodists—when I was a kid. We had a kind of tent house, with a solid roof and canvas walls. I guess that must have been my first encounter with this place. I would slip over to the Strand whenever I could, even then. I walked over to the Camp the other day to look at the place where we stayed. All the canvas houses look about the same. I think that ours was on a street called Bethany Way."

At the word "Methodist," Gates had turned to look at Todd, and their eyes had met in mild surprise as if each was finding out something previously unknown about the other.

"We were Methodists too," Gates said. "In Leestown, Pennsylvania. The statistical probability was fifty-fifty that you would be a Methodist and the same that you would be a Baptist. The difference was that the Baptists had bigger revival meetings and the Methodist preacher wore a robe."

It seemed to Scriber that for all of Gates' effort to appear detached about this, he was more involved in what he was saying now than in anything that had happened that day on the beach or this evening at dinner.

He went on. "We had our own Sunday night youth group and then met ecumenically at the drive-in. By the time we got out of high school, there had been a lot of crossing of the lines, so to speak, and usually the boy joined the girl's church when they got married, except for the fanatics. It seemed to come out about even, and the fresh blood was good all around."

Gates was enjoying himself. "I remember one of my friends who was going to marry a Baptist. I went to see him baptized on a Sunday evening. They went down into a big tank of water with a picture of a river behind it, lit by fluorescent lights. The preacher had his right hand in the air and was saying some words. Then all I saw of Edwin was his rear end. He was about 6' 3", and he told me later that he had thought the way to be baptized in the Baptist Church was to put your whole head under water. He had never witnessed a baptism. Did he ever look funny when the preacher made him stand up, his head dripping wet, and start all over again.

I was sure that he wished he had stayed a Methodist."

Scriber had noticed that both young men had used the past tense in speaking of being Methodists. At the same time he got the strong impression that they were still pretty close to the experiences they had described. It seemed many of the people he knew felt a strong ambivalence about their religious background.

He certainly would not define himself in relation to the small-town church in which he had grown up, but at a good many parties the subject surfaced. The Galley seemed an unlikely setting for such a conversation, but it was not the first time that food and drink had turned the talk to religion. Perhaps here it was all the stained glass or the candles in wine bottles, usually those squat Almaden ones covered with the accumulated drippings of a thousand nights. Whatever the immediate cause of these associations, it was not unusual for highly sexual situations to evoke religious emotions in him, and in the same way, religious occasions were often charged with sexual overtones. Perhaps sex and religion were the last holdouts of a sense of awe, of an awareness of mystery in life, of the possibility of being overwhelmed by something outside oneself.

"Funny, but you can hardly find a sexier place than a church youth group," Scriber said. He spoke in a way that revealed that he had thought about this before; there was something of the lecturing professor in it.

"Dorie and I"—he turned toward Gates and added, "She's my girlfriend—were driving home from the Ruston flea market one Sunday. You know the old road that is now pretty much a commercial strip: hamburger joints, gas stations, and now a couple of those massage parlors. The Coliseum is on that road, and across from it is the Coliseum Motel and next to that a Baptist Church, red brick colonial with white columns and a green lawn. I'm sure that when the church was built, houses with trees and grass lined that road. But there we were, surrounded by pavement and neon signs, hungry and wanting to get home to have a closer look at the old church pew that I had bought to put out on my porch.

The church service had just let out as we stopped at a light. The older people were on the porch, and out under the trees the teenagers were standing around; patterns of pairing off were apparent. The girls wore short skirts—that seems to be fine at church now—and the boys had on slacks and shirts that looked as though they had been ironed by their mothers. They all looked washed and healthy, shining hair and polished shoes, the sort of kids you would notice if they were walking down the street of a city like New York or Philadelphia. They signaled clean habits and clean air. And you could just tell that they would go home from church and have a good Sunday dinner and a lazy afternoon and then gather again that evening at a meeting of the parish youth group.

"I said to Dorie, 'Sexy, isn't it?' She wasn't sure it was that or just the relief of seeing people under a tree on a green lawn rather than all that endless pavement and quick-food clutter. The light changed, and as we drove away I tried to imagine all those Christians—the boys full muscled and graceful even in a slouch, and the girls looking like ripe peaches—being thrown to the lions at the Coliseum Motel."

Coffee always did that to him, made him talkative and sometimes even high. Had he been a little higher, he might have gone on to say that he had hoped deep down that the Christians would win, that the Church, or someone, could figure out a way to keep that fresh-faced sexy innocence that he had seen at 12:10 on a Sunday morning. He had caught a glimpse of himself there at that age, living in a simple protected world of religious feeling as warmly felt as adolescent lust and as full of high hopes and sweet pain.

He had come a long way from then, tramping around on Sunday morning with a woman who was not sure, and about whom he was not sure, bargaining with people who spent their Sunday mornings selling the leftovers of the past, then coming home with an old pew made by some rustic carpenter from some poor black church, which he would put on the porch of a house which thus far he had only dreamed of and toward which he had not driven the first nail.

Scrib continued. "The old pew has a hand-carved shield on each end, placed to protect God's children from every peril. When we reached the apartment, after picking up some hamburgers that came out so quickly that they must have been ready-made, we put the pew out on the deck and speculated on the dealer's story that the old bench had been hand-made by black people trying to imitate the fine pews of the white church in town.

"Dorie pointed out the amateurish detail, lovingly executed. 'Can't you just see those people in the evening, after working all day, trying to imitate the woodwork which one of the women in their church cleaned and polished for the white folks every week. She probably took one of the men in there one day and he made a sketch of that design on the armrest— those diamond medallions. Notice, Scriber, it's not a true diamond. He did it freehand. These days that old pine is even harder to find than the walnut they copied.'

"She pointed out, too, how the seat and the back were curved. 'Those black people used to spend the day at church; some still do. They wanted to have pews like the white folks, just as they try to straighten their hair. But when it came right down to it, they made the bench for comfort. If you couldn't sit on it for three hours, it wouldn't do in their church. As our maid at home used to say, they didn't just zip in and zip out; they liked to "linger with the Lord." Did black people "linger" at sex the way they did at religion because of quite a different way of giving oneself up to time and history and suffering and ecstasy?'

"You could actually settle back in that old pine pew. Dorie had seen that too."

"Todd had joined us on the porch later on. You put your two cents in, remember? You said you thought I was out of my mind, spending forty dollars on it but you conceded that I got a good buy. I remember your comment: 'Have you noticed that you sort of sit in this pew rather than just perch on it? I like it.'

"And so we sat there for a long time that Sunday, reading the paper and saying a dozen times, if we said it once, that I had got a bargain."

The boy in jeans and tee shirt put the check on the table, and they divided it three ways. Todd paid Gates' part and left what seemed to Scriber a large tip. As they walked toward the door, Gates stopped at the same table they had visited on the way in.

Scriber and Todd waited for him on the boardwalk, now more crowded than ever. A stiff breeze fanned Todd's cigarette bright red, and the smoke blew away instantly. The sky was clear and, despite the bright lights, Scriber could make out two or three stars. Neither he nor Todd spoke, Todd simply enjoying his cigarette and both of them taking in the scene. The time and place were rich with variety—of color and smells and people, straight and flamboyant—and thick with the sounds of the amusement park and the sea and a thousand feet drumming on the boardwalk.

Gates joined them.

"They want us to come over to their place. It's that big brown shingle up the beach, just where the boardwalk stops."

He was obviously talking to Todd, who looked quickly at Scriber and was clearly uneasy.

"We'll see. Maybe we'll drop by later on, OK?"

Gates didn't answer, perhaps as surprised as Scriber at the paternalism in Todd's voice. Not entirely sure that the invitation had not included him but sensing that Todd was assuming that it had, Scriber pleaded weariness and said that he would be going back to the motel. "I've got a good book, and I may get up early tomorrow to do some beach combing. One of my nephews collects shells."

There was the usual protest, but it was pro forma. They said good night and Scriber walked up the boardwalk toward the Holiday Inn, glancing back once to see them still talking in front of the restaurant. Then they turned and walked away in the opposite direction, toward the amusement park.

CHAPTER

18

The Strand Auction occupied a large storefront, not far from his motel. The crowd had spilled over onto the boardwalk. He stopped to see what the auctioneer was selling. The man wore a white shirt and tie, suspenders, and had a round, worried face. He was holding up a large gilt-edged pitcher, and though Scriber could not see it, he knew that there was a washbowl to go with it.

He had actually washed with a bowl and pitcher when he was a boy. His great-grandmother had one, plain white, on the back porch off her kitchen with a towel hanging on a nail above the bowl. She filled the pitcher before each meal at the pump in the kitchen sink, and for the men who needed to shave in the morning, she would heat water on the stove and fill the pitcher from the kettle.

Now those pitchers and bowls had become collectors' items. Scriber had even had punch out of one at a faculty party. As he walked away from the edge of the crowd, the bid for the pitcher was at $42.

He was not in his room more than ten minutes. He came out wearing a duck jacket and deck shoes. He crossed the street and turned right on the boardwalk, toward the pavilion and what he now knew to be Sea Camp. He walked more deliberately than most of the people out at that hour, as if he knew where he was going.

Every horse on the carousel had a rider. It was a particularly beautiful carousel. The horses were painted in gay colors and each one was unique, highly individual in the position of the legs and the expression of the head. The calliope was loud, and in another context the music, like the colors, would have seemed raucous and gaudy. But altogether—the movement of the horses up and down and round and round, the sense of abandon exhibited by the adults who were at liberty to ride by virtue of having children, the delight of the spectators—the sight seemed to Scriber surpassingly beautiful, even poignant.

He had stopped to watch for a moment, long enough to notice two details he could easily have missed. Above the carousel, around the canopy, were oval stained-glass windows the size of a birdbath. They glowed softly, by no means competing with the whirling and pulsating lights below. In alternate windows were the facemasks of comedy and tragedy, more subtly differentiated than he was accustomed to seeing, in old high school auditoriums, for example. The one seemed to smile rather than to laugh, and the other to ask a question rather than grimace.

Scriber walked around the carousel to the lake side where the carnival ended and the lagoon stretched dark and silent toward the quiet town beyond. The faces, from that side, glowed more brightly and their expressions were more distinct. It was there, too, that Scriber saw, at the end of the line waiting to ride, Todd and Gates. Todd was holding two tickets. They stood with their backs to Scriber, and there was something in the way they stood which recalled to Scriber the paternal tone in which

Todd had spoken to the younger man earlier.

He walked across the pavilion, and immediately the sounds of the carnival were muffled. A fold-up billboard stood in the middle of the boardwalk, just beyond the main entrance of the pavilion:

GREAT PREACHING BY THE SEA
10:30 a.m. — Matthew Moore
7:30 p.m. — Christopher Matick
IN THE GREAT TABERNACLE

He was almost alone. No one was on the sand, which featured at intervals signs reading: NO BATHING ON SUNDAY. There were a few solitary strollers, an occasional jogger, and a few quiet couples—quite young or quite old—sitting facing the sea. Something, of which he was vaguely aware, seemed to be missing, but he could not say what it was. "It feels dark here," he thought.

As he reached the long park, he saw the cross, glowing blue-white. He turned away from the beach and walked slowly. People sat on the dark front porches of every house he passed, like chickens gone to roost. He could smell flowers—roses and the soapy fragrance of geraniums.

He crossed two little side streets before he came to Bethany Lane where the dim streetlight made the sign barely visible. There the boarding houses gave way to small tent-like cottages with postage stamp front yards. One of the occupants displayed an American flag large enough for a post office. The porches, none of which could accommodate more than three or four chairs, were crowded with residents sitting not more than six feet from the sidewalk.

Scriber could almost feel the curiosity in the air as he

passed, as if no one walked this way alone at night. Conversations would stop as he approached, and start again, in the same low tones, after he had passed. That, he knew, was the country way. It was not just curiosity, but a certain attentiveness to the stranger, which on certain occasions took the form of a healthy concern. That was the irony of it, that the moral seriousness which was left over from an earlier Puritanism produced an oppressive moralism. Scriber felt uncomfortable under those quiet, searching eyes, so close to listening ears and silent tongues. In the daylight, or in a time of real, demonstrable need, that same attention would be perceived in quite a different way. As he passed another block, even the sweet odor of petunias seemed heavy, almost oppressive.

He turned away from the canvas houses toward the central park. Now he could see that the cross was on the face of a lopped off but very high spire. Actually the spire was more like a turret, with the proportions of an inverted ice cream cone. A fountain splashed, and he found a bench facing the building. He could not make out the detail of the tabernacle, but it was massive, reaching almost the whole width of the park and seeming to spread its wings like a mother hen toward the tent houses which surrounded it on three sides. To the right of the fountain was the statue of a man who seemed to be giving a speech, and to the right of the statue was a circular pavilion, like a large gazebo, surrounded by tall flowers which he was sure were hollyhocks. The lights glowed over the roofs of the large houses. Scriber sat listening to the distant sound of the carousel while the moon rose golden in contrast to the blue-white light that glowed above the park.

CHAPTER

19

It seemed a long time ago, as he thought about it, that he had first gone to New York as a student. He still had the most vivid picture of the iron work in the high roof of Penn Station and the softness of the light on the autumn day when he arrived, full of the unlimited hopes of a man in his mid-twenties. Then, it had seemed to him that he could do anything he wished and become whatever he chose.

He had studied hard during the weeks leading up to Christmas break. He was not going back to Oklahoma for the holidays. His parents had sent him money for the theater, and he planned to see the city, for which he had had little time that fall. He would be in New York only one year, and he and his parents had decided that it was the reasonable thing for him to do that Christmas.

On the Friday before the holiday he had gone to City Center, to see *The Nutcracker*. It began to snow early in the afternoon and he had gone first to Fifth Avenue and walked up and down for hours, looking at the animated windows. He enjoyed being in the crowd after the months of relative isolation as a student.

When he noticed the time, he realized that he would have to find supper after the performance, though he had eaten the evening meal after seven o'clock only a few times in his life. By the second intermission he was very hungry, and in looking around for the concession stand, he had caught the eye of a woman looking directly at him. He had played the shy boy and bought himself an orange drink and returned to his seat, but not without curiosity.

It was well after ten o'clock when he finally had a sandwich and cake at a little place not far from the theater. He was just finishing his coffee, which tasted good on that cold night that steamed the windows of the little cafe, when she came in, now wearing a black, curly fur coat over her red dress. She did not see him right away, and he looked at her closely as she took a table not far from his. She was not yet thirty, but older than he, with dark hair and the fresh face of someone who has time for good food, sleep, and grooming. He had not thought her especially pretty, but she was intriguing. He liked the straightforward way in which she pulled up her own chair and ordered immediately without opening the menu. She obviously knew the place.

She lit a cigarette and then, with a slight tilt of her head as she shook the match out, she looked toward him. He had not looked away in time, and she caught his eye and smiled. When his check came, he picked it up and walked, his coat over his arm, to her table as if he were on his way to the cash register.

"Hello," he said, "I saw you there. Did you like the performance?" He was feeling awkward, particularly since the waiter had come with her pastry and coffee.

"May I join you?" he asked.

She pulled the cup closer to her and without looking

at him said, "Yes, yes, of course. Are you new in the city?"

He ordered a second cup of coffee. He could tell that she knew he had never been to the ballet before that night. She talked at length about what was done well and poorly, and he had been able at least to say that he thought the unfolding Christmas tree was a technical achievement.

Then she had invited him to her place for a nightcap, suggesting that her apartment was on his way uptown. They came in out of the wind which had risen after the snow became finer. At first it had been like being at home. A Christmas tree helped create an especially welcoming feeling in the small space. She played some Christmas music on her phonograph, and after a second drink of something hot that tasted a little like lemonade, she had slipped off her shoes and so did he.

When he woke up, she was asleep and the room was very quiet, the world outside muffled by the snow.

He came down the stairs quietly, like a boy coming home too late. He had seen the cross when he was halfway down the last flight, through the window above the old brownstone's front doors. It glowed white with blue edges, and under it were the words, also in neon, "Jesus Saves." He hadn't seen it when they came in, their heads ducked against the wind, she holding his arm. He turned quickly down the deserted street, wishing that he had not given her his name and address.

For weeks after that, when he rode the subway and passed the 86th Street stop, he knew that he could easily get off and find the house just by the cross on the Pentecostal Church across the street. But he always sat very still and read

his newspaper intently until the doors had closed.

Three weeks later, when everyone was back at the dormitory and he was near the end of exams, someone down the hall had called him to the phone. "Some woman, Scrib."

The voice was not one he recognized.

"We were at the ballet together, before Christmas. Remember? You came up to my place."

He had tried to put it out of his mind, but yes, he remembered.

"How are things with you?" he said distantly.

"Not so good. That's what I called about. You should go to see a doctor; you know what I mean. I've just found out, but I probably had it when you were here. I'm sorry, especially if it was your first time."

He had thanked her for calling him, as if he had just been invited to dinner. He just sat there, in the closet that served as a phone booth for his floor, until someone banged on the door and yelled, "Hey, that's a phone booth, not a chapel."

Then he had taken a shower, long and hot, and put on clean clothes. As he left the room, his roommate looked up from his desk. "Who is she, Scrib?"

"No one you would know," he had answered.

The university library looked like a temple, and the reference room was an inner sanctuary with high cathedral-like windows. Soft light fell on long mahogany tables where a dozen or more people had distributed themselves like so many monks hunched over in prayer. He found the book he

wanted and sat down at the table farthest from the door.

She had called it "the big S," and he learned that the symptoms were rash and a sore which developed six to ten weeks after infection. If not arrested, the disease could lead to insanity and death, but "since the advent of penicillin, syphilis seldom reaches its more extreme stages." He sat with the book open, staring at the line drawing of the coiled spirochaete, trying to discern by some inner probing whether it was even now in his bloodstream, a Christmas gift from the great city to a boy from Oklahoma who had not known its name or shape until today. Even now it might be spiraling through his veins until it erupted one fine morning as he was dressing to go to class, or perhaps he would feel the sore as he tossed in his sleep in the middle of the night.

As he came down the steps, it was quite dark. Lights were on in the chapel, a small baroque building at one corner of the quadrangle. A few students were going that way, and he followed. A poster at the door announced, HOLY COMMUNION–6 p.m. Inside, he smelled the clinging odor of incense from an earlier service; the fragrance seemed to him sweet and clean, like a newly swept house. On the altar, eight candles flickered, illuminating the face of a stylized crucifix. As he knelt, following the lead of others more familiar with the chapel, his eyes fixed on the wound on the side of the crucified Jesus. His finger went to his lips and he prayed, 'Have mercy on me.'

The service followed the prayer book, and at the right time he went to the communion rail, which had always seemed as strange as the common cup might be to a Baptist. As the student next to him tipped the cup to her lips, he suddenly felt a numbing fear: should he drink from the cup? Could he infect someone that way? But the priest was in front of him, saying, ". . . preserve your soul and body unto everlasting life." He took the cup. When he was back at the pew, kneeling down with others who had eaten and drunk, he found himself repeating, 'preserve my body and soul. . . .'

Two weeks later, early on a Tuesday morning, when looking in the mirror, he discovered a sore on his lip, just at the corner on the left side. It was not large, more like an angry pimple, but the book had said that the canker could be so small as to go unnoticed. He had been checking himself so carefully—locking himself in one of the stalls—that a louse would not have gone undetected. Now it had come, fiery and vindictive, in a place for all to see. He shaved carefully and said to his roommate as he dressed, "Stan, will you take notes for me in seminar this morning? I've got to see someone."

He had waited two hours at the outpatient clinic, and when the young intern finally saw him and asked him what the trouble was, the doctor paid no attention to the sore growing on his mouth. His questions were perfunctory: "Is the woman married? Has she notified all her contacts? Have you had any relations with anyone else in the intervening time?" Then he simply walked out and a nurse came in to take blood from his arm.

As he sat holding his thumb on the cotton ball, she said:

"We'll know about this in a couple of days. In the meantime, the doctor wants to give you the penicillin series, all in one shot, for your protection. Let's put that in the other arm."

As he rolled down his sleeves, she said, "We'll call you, probably on Thursday."

It made him feel strange to know that the doctor had talked the situation over with her. "By the way," she said, "you should get something at the drug store for that cold sore."

The number to call was on his desk when he came from lunch on Thursday. The secretary at the hospital said, "Please hold on, Mr. Newall. I have a message here from Dr. Forbes." She seemed to be shuffling through some papers. "Yes, here it is. Test negative. Thank you for calling. Good-bye." He had lain down on the bed and cried, grateful that his roommate was not there.

For the rest of that semester he had gone to the Baptist Church on Broadway. The minister was an old-fashioned preacher who labored over biblical texts, and the congregation seemed a remnant of middle-class respectability. He began to go to an airy cafeteria near the church for Sunday dinner. They had roast beef every Sunday, and the rolls reminded him of his mother's. Occasionally he would eat with people from the church, and they would talk about the sermon, as his parents did. Toward the end of the term he had missed a few Sundays; he was busy at school. But that year, from February to April, he could be seen on most Sunday mornings in a white shirt and his grey suit, walking down Broadway before eleven and returning with the Sunday papers in mid-afternoon.

When he moved to Collegemont, he had joined the Presbyterian Church. But he soon discovered that his need for the church was not the same as it had been in the city. There he had needed order and discipline, protection from the city's anonymity and unlimited possibilities. The situation in Collegemont was far from that. If anything, life there was too ordered and routine, circumscribed by the duties of a new professor and the provincialism of small-town mores. So he had begun to play tennis on Sunday mornings, and it seemed to him now that not going to church provided the same liberation that the well-starched congregation in uptown New York had given him during that late winter and spring.

He had never returned to 86th Street, and he did not call. He had wondered about her and had considered writing to thank her for letting him know. But there was something in him that did not want to touch her again, even in a letter. He had tried more than once to remember what she looked like. But what kept coming to his mind instead was the quietness of that night and how he had come down the stairs on tiptoe and seen that neon cross right across from her place and how he had walked down the middle of the street to the subway stop making new tracks in the snow, not looking back once.

CHAPTER

20

The moon had risen higher and the fountain splashed. It was the movement of two people who had been sitting in the gazebo that roused Scriber from his thoughts. The couple came from the far side of the pavilion, and as they walked to the door, the man's hand was around the young girl's waist. They seemed not to notice Scriber as they stood just outside the doorway, flanked by what Scriber could now see were in fact hollyhocks. As they stepped into the moonlight, Scriber recognized the tall young man in Holiday Inn blue who had been tending the pool that morning. And the girl was the one who had waited on him at lunch. They sat down on the wall of the flowerbed.

The splashing water was now catching the moon and breaking it into a thousand shining fragments. The sound of the water fell gently into the pool in which Scriber thought he could see the flash of goldfish. Then the man spoke, in a voice that was both soft and earnest.

"Neither place seems quite right, Ruthie. Sometimes I think they are too much alike. But this side is at least healthful, and a lot less expensive. Boy, what people will pay for a jazzy dining room and a meal that's more gimmick than food. We could eat at the *Bread of Life* for a week on what people spend on one meal over in the Strand."

Then, after a little pause, the girl spoke. "Listen, Mark, you can hear the carousel. Funny, hearing it from this side." Then they seemed to be just sitting there listening to the music.

"You know what I like best about this place?" he asked. "I knew it the day we got here, what it was going to be like. I walked into my room—it was late afternoon and we had been driving all day—I walked into the room and someone had opened the window toward the ocean. A breeze was blowing the curtains, white curtains, and not one thing in that room shouldn't have been there. There was, Ruthie, a bed, with a white bedspread that was no more than a kind of crinkly sheet, and it had been patched. There was one pillow, an empty chest of drawers, a table, a chair, and a lamp. That was it. Not even an ashtray. And no Gideon Bible, as if they expected you to have your own. I've never been in one, but it seemed to me like entering a monastery. The room sort of said poverty, chastity, obedience, but it wasn't the hair shirt type of monastery. I knew that the sheets on the bed would be white and smooth, and that they would feel as cool and white as milk in a spring house."

Scriber was surprised that someone his age would even know what a spring house was.

The girl seemed content to listen––perhaps she was enjoying the soft sound of the carousel—and he went on.

"Then we went to supper. Remember? It was the same way. The place had lots of windows, not like that den of a restaurant where we work, and the food was plain. I remember that we had lots of real bread and butter, and the vegetables were great, served just straight but not bland. I knew right then that I would like it. It's as honest as milk and honey, and that peanut butter that is just peanuts that we get at the *Bread of Life*."

He paused as if waiting, and then said, in a more musing tone, "I've been trying to figure out what it all has to do with a camp meeting."

"Well, I guess," she answered, "that everything really good has something to do with the good news."

Ruthie spoke in the same mood, softly and without showing any effort to convince him or herself.

"Do you remember the text that Matthew Moore preached on, last week, from Isaiah, I think: 'Why do you spend money for that which is not bread, and your labor for that which does not satisfy?' Maybe food and work and how you dress yourself, and your room, are all part of the good life. Real freedom means seeing that and not getting hung up on this or that so that it becomes some kind of idol."

"Look," he said, "who's going to be the preacher around here?" She laughed, and he pulled her up by both hands.

They both saw Scriber at the same time. As they came around the pool, Scriber spoke first to the man who Scriber could now see was in his twenties: "I hope you don't have to clean that pool too early in the morning." Then, seeing that the man did not recognize him, he added quickly, "I'm staying at the Holiday Inn."

"Oh, hi," the girl said, "we didn't see you there. Nice night, isn't it? I told you about my friend. This is Mark Furlson."

They shook hands and Mark said, after a short, awkward pause, "We don't work tomorrow; it's our day off. We were just going back to the house."

Scriber could see that they were walking back in the direction from which he had come. Before he could suggest it, the girl had asked if he was going their way.

"Sure, I'll walk along with you. I'm ready to get back to the Strand."

"What brings you to the Camp?" the girl asked.

Scriber explained that he had never heard of Sea Camp before today, and that he had just been out for a walk and happened that way. They invited him to the service the next day.

"I think I'll take advantage of this last chance at the beach," he said.

They said goodnight in front of a large old house with urns of white petunias and rocking chairs on a long front porch. They didn't repeat their invitation to come to the Camp the next morning. Theirs was quite a different kind of earnestness from that of the young men he had overheard earlier in the evening.

As he walked back toward the bright lights, he imagined Mark going up to his room where he was sure the bed would be made with a worn white spread. This young man would say his prayers before he crawled between the cool white sheets.

The line at the carousel was even longer than before, though there were fewer children at this hour. He walked on past the leaping horses and the glowing faces without slowing his pace. Near the Ferris wheel the bumper cars were careening wildly, urged on by people laughing and shouting hysterically as they slammed into each other like the drunken pigs inebriated on his uncle's overflowing home brew hidden in one of the pig houses.

He did not stop at his motel, but walked on past the auction, now dark, to the more dimly lighted northern end of the strand. At the end of the boardwalk he leaned against the railing and listened to the sea.

To his left, facing the beach, was a large brown-shingle house. The front door was open, and in the wide front hallway a white paper lantern glowed as softly as the moon that was now lighting a path on the ocean. There were people on the porch. He could see someone in cream-colored linen trousers, moving back and forth in a swing. Two people sat on the steps, looking out across the deserted beach, and several others sprawled in low chairs. Every few minutes someone would go inside, the screen door would bang behind him, and soon he would reappear with a glass in his hand. The upstairs windows of the house were dark, and the rooms downstairs were dimly lit, as if by candlelight.

The longer Scriber stood watching the house the more he was aware of the banging of the screen door and the flickering of light in the upstairs windows. At infrequent intervals a flash of light would appear in one of the windows, as if someone had opened a door from a lighted hallway and then closed it quickly, or had switched on a bedroom light and then closed the door immediately so as not to disturb someone sleeping.

Then, as Scriber stood in the darkness at the end of

the boardwalk, two men came into clearer view. The man in creamy pants stopped swinging and came down the steps. He seemed to look in Scriber's direction, and then he walked out onto the beach, in a straight line from the house toward the lifeguard's tall chair and the boat that lay upside down beside it. It was Gates. Scriber recognized him by the pants and the way he walked, with a kind of energy, like the bouncing ball in the sing-alongs. He stopped a few yards from the wet sand and stood looking out to sea. Scriber did not move, though the most natural thing would have been to speak and walk across the beach toward the young man. It was just light enough that either man could have recognized the other, but dark enough for both to pretend not to.

Gates sat down on the sand. Scriber was on the verge of moving in Gates' direction—he may even have sent the first command to his muscles to do so—when another figure came across the beach, almost startling Scriber by the silent way in which he approached the seated figure. Whoever it was, he did not speak at all but simply sat down and looked out to sea. Scriber felt strangely like an intruder, and more so when he recognized the second man. It was Mark.

Back in his room, he turned the air conditioner off and opened the door to the balcony. He removed the orange bedspread and put it under the bed. Then, naked as a boy at an Oklahoma swimming hole, he stretched his body between the white sheets. He listened, but he could not hear the carousel, only the steady wash of the sea. He was almost asleep when he thought of something. He reached first into the drawer beside the bed, but it wasn't there. Then he went from drawer to drawer, moving naked in the dark, until his hand hit it. He walked to the balcony, and standing in the moonlight with the Gideon Bible, he said out loud: "They didn't expect me to have one of my own." He laid the book on the table and was soon asleep.

CHAPTER

21

A s always, he woke up early. The salt air was heavy in the room, and the sheets felt cool. He had slept all night without waking, and even now wasn't what you would call awake. But somewhere between waking and sleeping, he could see and feel the old man so close to him that he wouldn't have been surprised if he had jumped up from the foot of the bed to tell him that his grandmother would skin them both if they didn't get the chores done and wash up for breakfast.

Twelve hundred miles from the place where he began, as far east as he could go, waking up alone in the Holiday Inn, he could hear his grandfather's words, as he did on many of the mornings of his life: "When your eyes open, put your feet on the floor." There was in those words something at once reprimanding and cajoling, joking and helping. Sometimes the old man had added, after Scriber had reached his teens and his grandfather, or anybody, slipping into the room while he was asleep couldn't help seeing that the boy under the sheet was becoming a man, "When it gets up, wake up, and when you wake up, get up."

Like a passage from the Sermon on the Mount or the communion service, or perhaps even better, Chaucer, the words had stayed in his mind, tied to his very physiology and

114

to the daily act of waking up. The words had stayed, as both law and grace, both at once, and he was on just about any morning of his life as likely as not to hear his grandfather's voice with the first sensation of waking, whether in the old iron bed which he had painted white when his grandmother gave it to him or here in this motel room where nothing knew his name. It tended always to happen on momentous days.

The Cherokee-gentle sheriff used to sneak into Scriber's room, like one of their forebears stalking game in the woods of North Carolina or Georgia. He would get down on all fours at the foot of the bed to wait for the clothespin he had put on the boy's ear to wake him up. Scriber had first met the world on many of the mornings of his boyhood with the mixed sensations of pain and laughter, his ear throbbing and his grandfather, six-feet four and silver badge already pinned on, giggling at the foot of his bed. The boy had only to stir and the man was there to rub the smarting ear and rouse him for a little work and for his grandmother's grand breakfast. On other days the old man—funny, that's how he was, an old man, but he hadn't seemed so at the time and wouldn't seem so now—would tickle his nose with a chicken feather. He had been out to gather the eggs. Or he would just whisper in his ear: "How's my punkin' eater?" or "How's your hammer hangin'?" And they would go to do a little work at the old barn and come in to breakfast together: oatmeal, fried eggs that he had just gathered, their own ham, and her big crusty biscuits with their butter and wild honey. His grandmother would get a kiss, or a pinch, and the boy would wonder, later on, how he woke her up.

There was in this memory some great thing which he

had felt himself losing (or perhaps he had never fully grasped and yet was trying to keep and to understand), some lost wholeness and fullness, the richness of that home where people worked hard and had stern views about the importance of doing so, but where even the realities of supporting a family in the depression didn't turn their days into drudgery or their bodies into machines. His grandfather, keeping a farm going and kindly harassing the bootleggers, waking him with clothespins and feathers, helping his grandmother with the dishes even though the sink was too low for him, never failing to notice that the little woman who spent most of every day in an apron was still a woman and that behind her protests she liked being pinched, even while doing the dishes, which for her was a sacred activity. Something profound rested in the old man teaching a sleepy boy to get out of bed, thus filling even the sense of duty with sex and life and the humor of being alive.

Scriber looked down at his body from the height of two pillows emblazoned with the words "Holiday Inn" where his grandmother would have embroidered flowers like the lilacs outside his window, and tried to understand all that was in it.

"Good morning, punkin' eater," he said out loud, surprised by the depth of his voice. He stretched, one arm up and one down, like an airport flagman getting a big plane under way, and in the same movement reached for his watch. It was eight o'clock.

He didn't find many shells on the beach, mostly some large scallops. He hadn't really expected to find any conches today, having seen footprints going in both directions. He walked up the beach, past the shuttered brown shingle house. It was as quiet as the beach and as the sea, which was now at low tide. A man was sleeping in the swing which did not move at all. The sun was high already, invading the porch. Behind the red geraniums in large white pots other people were sleeping on the porch floor. Several glasses and bottles were on the steps, and a pair of loafers, neatly aligned, lay on the sidewalk, their toes pointing toward the beach.

Scriber continued on up the beach, at a leisurely pace. He was near the state park and had sat down on a retaining wall to consider turning back when he saw Todd coming toward him from farther up the beach. He was barefoot, the trousers he had worn last night rolled halfway to his knees. He had not shaved and looked more or less like a man who had been driving cross country for two days, grooming himself in service station restrooms. He was walking slowly, looking down. A casual observer might have taken him for a somewhat lackadaisical beachcomber.

It was clear to Scriber, however, that Todd was not looking for shells but was rather deep in thought. As he considered avoiding the younger man by pretending not to see him, Todd looked up and caught his eye. Both surprise and genuine pleasure crossed his face. "Hi, Scrib," he called, raising one hand automatically. "I thought you would be out earlier."

Scriber answered by getting up from where he was sitting and starting toward Todd, who had quickened his pace.

"Good morning," Scriber said, "looks like only the tennis team is out this early."

They stood half facing, half turned out to sea.

"No shells up the beach, Scrib. Beachcombers are always out early for the big ones. I did find one small spiral that you might like." He reached into his pocket and handed Scriber a creamy orange shell. "You can give that to your nephew."

Scriber turned it in his hand and said, "Thanks, Todd, you've saved the day. Since when do you get up this early for anything but tennis?"

A brief silence ensued in which it was clear that Todd was deciding what to say. He looked down at the toe with which he was shoveling sand and said, with unexpected resolution: "To tell the truth, Scrib, I haven't been to bed, at least not to sleep."

Scriber had the uneasy feeling that Todd was about to tell him something that he did not want to know, or at least something which, given the nature of their friendship, should not be expressed. But Todd went on before any defenses could be thrown up.

"Gates is still over there at the house, sleeping it off. I guess I had hoped that this trip would be something different." Then, apparently undecided about what he should say, or if he should say anything more at all, he looked directly at Scriber and said, "I'll walk along with you, OK? I'm not really ready to go back."

They walked up to the state park and sat at a shaded picnic table, both on one side, facing the sea. Todd talked with the groggy abandon of a man who had gone without sleep and was not quite in control. The setting too—the deserted beach showing few signs of civilization—seemed to help him forget that he was with his professor in whose classroom he would soon be sitting again. There was in his voice and manner a bid for intimacy, at least the verbal intimacy that is inescapable when confessing face to face rather than in the prescribed limits set up by the Church—no question that there was about it the tone of confession.

Todd had known Scriber for three years, and had wanted to tell him. But he had not found the right time, or the right words. And he was not even sure that it was fair to tell him. At first he had been infatuated with Scriber himself, but now it was Gates.

"But he doesn't seem to care what I want. I'd like to have a home, like anyone else, and just live a normal human life with neighbors, in a real town, and friends over to dinner, and maybe even church on Sunday, who knows?" He had not looked at Scriber, and did not do so as he went on.

"But Gates is younger and he likes the bar scene and that group at the beach house. Don't misunderstand. I don't want to put them down. It's just that it's not for me. I'd like to share some history as well as a bed with a person."

Then he cried, his head down on the picnic table. Scriber did not speak, or even reach out to put his hand on Todd's shoulder. He just sat there, listening to the sobs die away until what remained was only the steady, soft breaking of the surf. Then he said, his hands folded on the table and his eyes fixed on them, "I think I understand, Todd."

The younger man stood up first, and they walked back down to the beach. Only then did Todd use the word.

"It really doesn't mean anything, Scrib, the word. I have more in common with many married couples with children than with lots of gay guys if you are talking about actual life-style and values."

He paused and sat on one heel and then, as they walked, he went on. "When I was in college, I lived with a guy named Peter for eighteen months. During a break I went home with him, to a farm in North Carolina where his mother lived in a house just down the road from her old home place. They were all church people, salt-of-the-earth Methodist country folks, as they say, and plainspoken. His grandmother and I got on great, from the first day when she got out her quilts and showed them to me. There was one on the bed in our room and I had told her right away how much I liked it. She liked me, everyone just took me right in, and I went back there several times.

"Well, Peter's aunt was talking with his mother one day. She had seen a program on television, about 'those people.' (Peter's mother knew about him, and was trying to make the best of what must have been hard for her.) For example, she just made it seem the most natural thing that we should have a room together when I was there.

"Anyway, the more the aunt talked, the more his mother's hackles got up. Finally she just asked straight out, 'What are you talking about, Gretchen, 'those people'?

"It was his mother who later told us all about it. Gretchen had answered, 'About homosexuals. Like Peter and Todd?'

"The mother was about to take her on; she didn't even like the way her sister had said the word "homosexual." But the old grandmother broke in and settled it. 'Gretchen, you listen to me. There is no such thing as homosexual!'

"According to Pete's mother that was the end of that. And you know, Scrib, grandma was right. There isn't. There are just people who try to make the best of what biology and history and even geography have given them. And that means all of us."

They had reached the brown house, and Scriber left him there. "If I don't see you around here today, Todd, I'll see you back at school. Let's have an early match soon. OK?"

Scriber walked back to the motel. He had been able to think of nothing to say beyond "I hope you find what you want, Todd."

It had been a new experience for him, not unlike, he thought, his white student suddenly realizing that he liked his black roommate, quite apart from all liberal causes or provincial bigotry. He had come to Scriber's office to tell him about it.

Scriber's own compartmentalized thinking had been shattered by that brief encounter on the beach. He was at once as confused and enlightened as a respectable middle class businessman who realizes for the first time that his long-haired son is talking sense. He had suddenly discovered that his son shared the same human longing that sent that father to the office every day, however removed either youthful protest or grown-up conformity might seem from love and joy. Like that businessman, driving down the street in his big car regarding with mixed animosity and envy the kids lounging on the street corner, Scriber had walked down the other side of the street.

He might have said the reason he had, at one level, avoided Todd, though they played tennis together twice a week, was perhaps to avoid something hidden in himself. But that morning he had been unable to defend himself, and the caricature of a gay man had become a vivid person in pain. And as a result Scriber felt, beneath the initial embarrassment and the vague anxiety that were connected with his professional responsibility for Todd, strangely light and almost buoyant. "I hope you get what you want, Todd," he said out loud, to himself, in the tone of a benediction.

CHAPTER

22

He was splashing water on his face, preparing to shave—he always shaved before showering—when the phone rang. It was Dorie. The tone of her voice told him that she had not called just to say good morning.

"Having a good time? Good. Mother and Daddy are driving home after lunch, and they said that they could drive me down there, if you want company. Are you coming home tonight?"

He hadn't planned to for sure, and he wasn't certain he did want company. But he said, "Sure, Dorie, come on down. We can spend the afternoon on the beach and go back tonight. Are you ready for the 'Bible belt' at the beach?"

He could hear her say in an aside to her parents, "Yes, he will be coming back tonight." She wanted to know what he meant by Bible belt.

"Wait and see," he said. I'll plan to be here later in the afternoon, after 4:00, shall we say?"

He ate breakfast and was on the beach by nine-thirty. He played in the soft Sunday morning breakers like a child at play in a field of poppies. Now, back on land, he lay on his back, spread-eagled under the gentle sun. The earth seemed to move beneath him, turning and rising at the same time, and he opened his eyes to see if the sky held steady.

He was dozing, almost asleep, when he heard bells, the sound of an electric carillon. The music seemed to come from the Camp and was clearly audible above the sound of the low breakers. The sea and the bells seemed to complement one another, the surf rising and falling, giving depth to the music which had about it a flat monotony, like someone repeating a well-rehearsed speech. But together, the repetitious surging of the sea and the high, clear bells moved him, lying wet and limp and vulnerable in the sun.

He knew the tune and the words: "Jesus, lover of my soul, let me to thy bosom fly." He lay perfectly still, letting the sun and water, the music and memory wash over and carry him. "While the nearer waters roll, while the tempest still is high." He knew the whole song by heart, and could have sung it right there, out loud, for all the people in swimsuits, greasing themselves up for the day. He rolled over on his stomach and scratched with one finger in the sand.

That was when it had really started. He and Dorie had gone to a faculty party at the home of his departmental chairman who lived in a large, pseudo-colonial house, one of those nondescript but pretentious boxy places with columns added later to simulate the ante-bellum style. When he saw such houses, he always expected to see a big sign, the Magnolia Motor Inn, or something like that. His chairman spoke of the acreage as "our little place out in the country," though they were just beyond the city limits.

The furniture, newly American, bought by the room and as coordinated as it was expensive, matched the columns.

The living room sported a white rug, white and gold furniture, and a fireplace which had never been used. Toward the back of the house was a long room with a round table and a fireplace, and a television set; that was in fact the room where the family did their living. The front room was more of a "parson's parlor," and even that Saturday evening few of the fifty or sixty guests ventured onto the white rug.

They had served artillery punch, a drink made by steeping, for 24 hours, a mixture of bourbon, rye and cognac with thinly sliced lemons. When cold it went down like your Baptist aunt's fruit punch, but you soon learned that it wasn't!

Scriber had been at similar Southern gatherings, and he warned Dorie as they were directed toward the punch bowl: "That stuff is insidious; looks like iced tea and tastes like lemonade. But watch out."

The afternoon was warm—it was just before the end of term—and the host was ubiquitous with pitcher in hand. Only the dean seemed to resist strongly. By the time some people were leaving to go to dinner, the lethal punch had justified its name.

Toward evening, as the punch bowl was still being replenished and the host was still filling cups, something quite unforeseen happened. The guests had somehow migrated to the large kitchen (the most hospitable room in the house), where two black women in white uniforms were making ham biscuits and beginning to wash cups. Scriber had not seen the women outside the kitchen, and even now they seemed, while surrounded by a score of highly animated and noisy academics, to inhabit a world of their own. Scriber was leaning against a cabinet, trying to figure out how to get to Dorie who was pinned against the refrigerator across the room by a young man who seemed to be telling her the story of his life. Scriber had himself heard one confession, in the hallway, which he was sure would embarrass the woman the next time she saw him on campus. Had she mistaken his white turtleneck for a priest's collar?

Then it began. One of the black women started singing, quite unconsciously, softly, as she washed cups and looked out the window toward the woods behind the house. He had not recognized the song, but someone standing near the sink had. Quite uninhibited now, the fortyish man had begun to sing along with the woman: "Blessed Assurance. . . ." The other black woman took it up in a strong voice, as if something was happening at this party in which at last she could participate. Though there were no hymn books in the kitchen—that would have been *too* early American—one guest after another joined in. The black woman kept on washing, the guests kept drinking, and the party ended after dark with two dozen academics, whom he had hardly heard mention religion, singing gospel songs as lustily as if they had been brought up, to the last one of them, on the old-time religion. They had all known the words to the songs that Scriber had thought he had forgotten but which had come back as easily as swimming on the first warm day in spring.

As they left, Dorie said, "That was insidious punch. Are you sure that wasn't the religion department?"

"I was surprised myself," he said. "They all knew those old songs. Even I knew them. I don't suppose it meant anything to most of them, possibly nostalgia, or maybe rhythm, but it did surprise me. Did you notice that the only people who didn't join in were the really young ones, the teaching assistants and instructors? And even they looked like they wanted to. At least they didn't go in search of another room."

Dorie was silent for a moment, more sober than he. "Well, it's pretty clear that most of the people over thirty had been to Sunday school back there somewhere, and if you scratched them, they would bleed Methodist or Baptist beneath those with-it clothes. The black women go to that little Baptist church near the apartments, I'll bet you anything."

Scriber escorted her to her side of the car—he didn't always do that, but he did today—then came around and got in.

Before he started the car, he said, resting on the wheel, "It was like an antique show, Dorie, or like that auction we went to. It took just the suggestion of that one woman starting to sing, like church bells ringing on Sunday morning when you are trying to sleep. Everyone there knew what was happening, like people seeing an old jar and bidding against each other for it just because they share a common past that gets hold of them. That really was something today. Can you picture those people going to church together!"

"Only if they had some of that punch," she answered, "to loosen them up enough to show that hidden part of themselves."

Scriber had not seen many of his colleagues during that summer, and those he did see did not mention the party unless he brought it up. "Quite a party we had at Paul's place," he had said, a question in his voice as he and the woman who taught American literature had coffee in the faculty lounge.

"Had you ever seen anything like it, all that singing?" she mused lightly. "That was some punch they had."

When it was mentioned, the tone had been the same. Scriber brought it up only two or three more times. He was not sure what it had been for him, or for Dorie. It was at least a source of curiosity that summer, though there was no one in his department to whom he could say that.

CHAPTER

23

The carillon had stopped, and now a large single bell was ringing in long, deep notes, like someone knocking slowly on a door. Scriber got up, squinting at the sun, which was now more than halfway between the horizon and its zenith. The beach was filling up as the sun blazed. The bell stopped ringing. Must be about 10:30, he thought as he reached for the suntan oil.

The carillon played again at noon, though he could not hear it so clearly now. The surf had been good for the game, and he had never enjoyed it more. The metallic notes of the carillon suited his mood, like Bach being played on an organ with rich upper notes.

He gathered up his things and started across the beach. He was hungry and had decided to go to the Camp to one of those big boarding houses where he was sure that Sunday dinner would be as old-fashioned as the singing and preaching that had undoubtedly gone on this morning. He hummed as he walked, the tune halting and jumping ahead to the rhythm of walking in deep sand. "Jesus, lover of my soul. . . ."

In his room he stood looking in the mirror, saying to himself, 'Jesus, *want* make you love. Jesus, want *make* you love. Jesus, want make *you* love.' He reached for the shaving cream. 'Jesus, want make you *love.*' He spurted lather in his hand. 'Pretty clear I'm on the make for something. Jesus, want make you love.'

He continued looking into the mirror, trying to recall another face lost in his past, a face that he sometimes saw in his sleep, or when he woke up too early in the morning, or when he happened on a photograph of himself in a high school annual or when his family, at Christmas or some such time, would get out the pictures of their life in Lincoln. 'What brought me down here anyway? How could I ever tell that gentle story?'

During the college's spring break, one fine day I returned to Lincoln and sat in my Grandmother Nina's kitchen polishing off a lemon meringue pie.

"Scriber, when you've finished your pie, let's go into my bedroom; I want to show you something, something I made. I know already that it's something you are going to like."

She opened her bedroom closet door. "Will you please reach down for me that long box on the top shelf?"

The box, tied with kitchen string, had a printed label, "Henry's Dress Shop," and penciled below was "Scriber." I could have guessed. Neatly folded inside was a multicolored quilt, which she spread over her bed.

"I made it big enough to be a bedspread." Three-inch Nassau-yellow flowers with dark centers were spread over a variegated field of color. I could have found in its material some pieces of an old shirt of mine or some pajamas.

"I pieced and quilted it for you, Scriber, stitch by stitch. It's called 'Black-eyed Susan.' My mother, your great-grandmother, Pearl, clipped the pattern for me out of the *Kansas City Star*. These old hands may not let me make another one. I may take up 'africans'—her word for the increasingly popular afghan (which I was grateful was not in the box!) Anyway I am going to give it to you when you finally get married."

There was a short pause, and then I said quietly,

"Grandmother, it's really a lovely gift, and all the more so for me, who has slept so many nights under your beautiful quilts. As for marriage, I've not begun to think about that, too busy, I guess. For now that is all up in the air. If there is going to be a wedding, for sure it will be a long time coming. If you are going to give that quilt to me, you should just do it."

She looked at me steadily but not quite inquisitively, "Well, alright," she said. "You can put it back on that top shelf where no one will bother it. Did you finish that pie?" She didn't ask what I meant by what to her was a pessimistic and gloomy forecast, nor did she ever ask.

Later that year, a long box with its printed label "Henry's Dress Shop" crossed out, arrived at my apartment for Christmas. Inside was a store-bought card: "Merry Christmas, Scriber, and love always, from your grandfather and me."

CHAPTER

24

It was one of the grandest of the Victorian houses facing the old park, which was now filled with people and absolutely devoid of cars. That was what he had missed but been unable to identify last night. The streets were lined with parked vehicles but not one automobile or motorcycle spoiled the quiet Sunday morning. None would move until Monday. Noisy vehicles were no more welcome in The Camp on Sunday than swimmers on the beach. If one listened, the dull whine of distant traffic was there, coming from the Coast Highway. But it was barely audible. It was a mighty Sabbath which Sea Camp kept, mighty and deep.

The high frame house had recently been painted grey, with white trim and a striped white and blue awning running the length of the porch. The dining room was obviously open to non-residents; thirty or forty people were informally lined up at the open red door above which a sign was simply lettered BEULAH.

That was the way with all the boarding houses. He had not seen the words "hotel" or "lodge" in the whole town, just "Nebo" or "Ruth" or "Zion," as if all of them were alike and anyone coming to Sea Camp would know what to expect. Tradition apparently did not require billboard elaboration.

Scriber found a high-backed rocker at one side of the porch. From there he had a clear view of the sidewalk and the street, which was for today a promenade. Hungry as he was, he would let the line grow shorter. As he rocked and watched the passing parade, he tried to isolate the factors which made it immediately apparent that these people were coming from church. He first decided that it was obviously the hour, nearly one o'clock on Sunday. Then he decided to bracket that factor, if possible, and look for the characteristics in the passersby themselves which evoked in him Sunday in Oklahoma, making him feel as if he had been to church himself and that he was part of this weekly ritual. He wondered if he stood out somehow, if all these people could spot some telltale posture or some subtle flaw which told them that he had not labored with them through hymn and prayer and sermon, that he was an interloper who had no right to this tranquil day and its feast of roast beef and fried chicken and warm apple pie.

His dress would not give him away. It was true that many of the women wore Sunday hats and among the men were many in dark suits. But there were also young men in short sleeve shirts, more carefully laundered than his. Everyone looked scrubbed; his own hair was still wet from the shower. Some were carrying bibles, and a woman near him held a dog-eared songbook titled "Gospel Gleanings."

He could hear the give-away language of church people. More than once he heard one man address another as "Brother so-and-so," and he even heard a middle-aged woman called "Sister." 'If the plural of brother is brethren,' he mused, 'do you call two women sistern?'

Some of the churchgoers were talking about the ser-

133

mon, though he could gather no idea of what it was actually about, just that about everyone had liked it. And occasionally someone would come down the sidewalk humming a tune, but he could not tell whether it was left over from the morning's celebration or just the expression of a hungry Christian looking forward to a good meal. More often than not, the songs sounded familiar.

So, none of this should have been strange to him. Though he had been to church only occasionally since graduating from high school and heading off to college in New York, this weekly ritual was still a vivid piece of his life's landscape. His paternal grandmother, Addie Belle Newall, had initiated him into the world of church.

At home, Addie Belle practiced the Christian faith in her own particular way. On every warm day she could be seen in her rocker on the long front porch of her home, on an elm-shaded street, reading the Bible, rocking in prayer, and greeting the neighbors. The porch was surrounded by chrysanthemums—she called them "Christmas anthems"—which smelled strongly like soap. Since Addie Belle had small place for housework, her soapy porch seemed quite ironic!

Three times a week she dressed up and walked four blocks to the First Baptist Church for the two services on Sunday and one on Wednesday evening. There Scriber, in singing hymns and joining in prayer, learned what it was to be part of a community.

Now Scriber recalled, once more, that summer Sunday, a communion day, when he noticed that the varnish was worn off of the top of the pew in front of Addie Belle, where she put her head and hands down after receiving the bread and grape juice. The only time she bowed in that way was on communion Sunday, when she would take hold of the pew with both hands and put her head down. Now as he rocked on this long front porch waiting for Sunday dinner, Scriber mused once more on that worn pew's evidence of the church's long history and what that meant for that praying woman. When I was baptized at age twelve, she told me that I could now join in communing every first Sunday, so I followed her lead. But I didn't continue in that ritual long enough to wear off any varnish.

But there was more. Quite apart from all those more or less obvious signals, something more profound was going on. Some might say, in a sociological mood, that these devout people passing by had effected a kind of social closure: they had observed the weekly habit of churchgoing and now they had the reassured feeling of a child who had done the last chores and was planning how to spend his allowance, or the adult who has put in eight hours and feels quite justified to while away the evening watching television and consuming too many calories. It would not have been difficult to see in the prosperous and decorous people going by, a smug self-satisfaction of social conformity.

A man was passing the Beulah now, in a suit that was just right—conservative in color with modest lapels but somewhat like what the English would call "trendy." There was about the man the look of a proprietor, both in his dress and in the way he seemed to marshal his family who walked beside and behind him. And projected in front of the entourage was a rather solemn face which seemed to announce, "We have been to church," and a portliness which announced as loudly, "and now we are going to enjoy our dinner."

Scriber thought for a moment that he was seeing the Protestant work ethic, so called, in microcosm: work hard and then enjoy, go to church and then enjoy yourself at Sunday dinner and have a long, lazy afternoon nap. You've earned it. And Monday get back to it, no nonsense.

Or if he had wanted to psychologize about that pious promenade, he could have heard evidence, and seen it as well, that churchgoing was for some an exercise in masochism. Two women passed by, both in rather stiff hats and equally stern faces.

"He certainly did step on our toes today," one said almost happily.

"Yes, he really told 'em."

These people had been at church since 10:30, and were only now coming to lunch. That, on a hot summer day, would be in the minds of most people masochism itself! And here were two women rejoicing in being told off by the preacher. Protestant penance!

But it was more even than mere habit or masochism that Scriber saw on that early Sunday afternoon. He saw, of course, scenes from his own boyhood; he saw the intimations of the possibility of fulfilling his own need for order and reas-surance—a boy coming home from church with his family on a Sunday, to savor his mother's ample cooking and their clean bright house. He had, it seemed to him, lived in that world for most of his life, at least until he was on the verge of thirty, a world in which chaos could be staved off by the decorous observance of habitual ways of thinking and acting, of ac-cepting and rejecting, by living in that ordered world which was still celebrated by approximately half of the American people every Sunday morning of the year. In moving from thirty toward forty he had traveled away from that world of the old certainties, both about himself and what he was and his infinite possibilities, and about the nature of the world.

As he sat there rocking, hungry but unwilling to move, he was not articulating these things; the words "order" and "chaos" may not have occurred to him at all. What he felt was a sense of something lost and not replaced, a vague longing that formed itself as a decided attraction to this place of old houses and elderly people and nostalgic young people. He felt all the while like an outsider, but sitting there rocking slowly back and forth and taking in the dappled day, he harbored, like a lone swimmer in a gentle sea, a secret and bittersweet pleasure.

Sunday morning at the Camp had about it the quiet of two spent lovers. That was the best he could do to frame an analogy. No doubt the people passing by would have been puzzled, perhaps even scandalized, to know what he compared their morning at worship to, and the subsequent lazy ease with which they approached this Sunday afternoon. But there it was, that look which he had seen, the opposite of all striving, the antithesis of pursuit and aggression. The most important part of this day had transpired, and what remained needn't be accomplished at all; it could only be accepted as what had already been given.

The mighty, deep Sabbath sustained a long lingering of the ecstasy which was at the heart of religion. However far these worshippers might be removed from that first enchantment of heartfelt religion, their Sunday worship was as perfunctory and routine as the regular Friday night coupling of those long married but whose youthful passion, still capable of flaring, most often takes the form of kindness or tenderness. It is always there, residual in the habitual observance of form just as newlyweds' ardor is, in the slow, easy movements, or the locking of fingers of an old couple in the middle of the night.

There was about the ambience of the time and place the surrender and acceptance of not speaking, of lying still, one's skin tingling under the finger of a lover with just enough energy to lift a hand to lazily caress, up and down, the other's back. How like the believer on the holy Sabbath, the lover who does not move or speak, resisting every impulse to repay or reward the silence and stillness, joy in its purest form. How rare it must be, that moment when striving stops and gifts are given and received like grace, and two people are simply together, asleep in each other's arms, or awake and yet as peaceful and still as sleep, like the landscape on which the sun has risen but where nothing yet is stirring.

Scriber—perhaps it was not more than his own mood—saw people going by who looked like lingering lovers, not so much walking as drifting, and when they spoke, it was in the low tones and with the economy of lovers who have been to some secret place in a time outside time. They could never tell you about it, in so many words, but it was there for anyone who had eyes to see.

CHAPTER

25

He went in to dinner. The dining room had been newly painted, white with yellow curtains. The long refectory tables wore plain white linen cloths. Half a dozen ice cream-parlor fans rotated lazily overhead, and between the high windows open to the garden potted palms moved in the breeze. Churchgoers sat at every table.

"May I join you?" he asked. The elderly woman across from him, who had pink cheeks and very blue eyes and looked like she had gone to bed before nine o'clock every day of her life, looked up at him.

"Sit down, young man. We were just about to say grace." And so they did.

He looked at his plate. He could hear the fan turning slowly above him, in the same rising and falling cadence of their prayer beseeching the Lord to make them truly thankful for the blessings they were about to receive and mindful of the needs of others, to bless the words they had heard this morning to their good.

Then they introduced themselves, the ones on his side of the table leaning over their plates to get a look at him. Everyone at the table was over fifty except himself and two teenagers at the other end.

The lady with the pink cheeks sat beside her husband, a thin-faced man in a black suit whom she introduced as "Mr. Stroud, who was a pastor at McMinnville for thirty-five years." Mr. Stroud was more interested in having his dinner than in conversation.

A couple in their early fifties sat between the Strouds and the teenagers. She wore rouge and a little round hat with a homemade red poppy that bounced on its long stem when she talked or ate. She had a prim little mouth, as if she shaped it by saying "sweet potato" or "Presbyterian" a hundred times a day. In telling any story she spared no detail whatever, and anyone could tell by looking at her placid, well-fed husband that he had long since given up trying to keep her on the subject, and that he, like the people at the table, learned to let her talk as background noise. They were, in fact, Presbyterians from the North taking their vacation at the Camp.

"My husband just has to get away from those four telephones in his office. We don't even have a telephone in our room here at the Beulah. Sometimes on Sunday at home we take the phone off the hook or go sit in the back yard where Harvey built a fish pool, back where we can't hear it ring."

The red poppy was bobbing wildly, like an antenna on a speeding police car. It is not clear whether she was speaking to herself, Mr. Barton, her husband—who was a willing listener—or to everyone at the table.

The teenagers were at Sea Camp for the day. It turned out that they were both in summer school at the University. The girl had sung at the service that morning, and the boy had driven her down. The boy looked slightly uncomfortable in a blue suit and tie, but when the food came, he joined Mr. Barton in forgetting the world behind a chicken leg.

The girl talked demurely with the couple across from her. As best as Scriber could tell, the balding man was an executive in one of the New York offices of the Methodist Church. His wife was stylishly dressed and spoke in low, careful tones. The people next to them must have been farmers. They reminded Scriber of his market lady and her husband. The man had said grace over his large rough hands as if he said that same prayer three times every day.

At first Scriber took the small lady next to him to be frail. He had noticed her hands folded on the edge of the table during the prayer; they were blue-veined and trembled slightly when she reached for the glass of water. But his impression changed when she spoke. The same slight tremor was in her voice, but she spoke with what he could only describe as presence. He listened carefully. What might have appeared to others as frailty was obviously only the necessity for wise husbanding of energy and words. She spoke with great economy, and the effect of that was not so much an impression of a grave weighing of words but of her real pleasure in being able to be there talking with him.

"How is life?" she asked Scriber. It was not the sort of opener he had expected, not that he had not heard the words or variations on them before. Even "Hi" and "Howdy" had no doubt degenerated from "How are you?" But from the little old lady in a navy blue dress and pearls which had taken on her own color, the words sounded strange. She could have been eighty years old, or even ninety. And she was not asking him how he liked the sermon that morning or where he was from or what he did, just "How is life?"

It reminded him of that time when his proud aunt had introduced him to her ancient black maid, Miss Clemmie. It had been shortly after he received his Ph.D.

"Clemmie, this is Dr. Scriber Newall."

The old woman had looked him straight in the eye and taken his hand between both of hers and pulled him down toward her.

"Hello, Scriber," she said in the deep voice of all mothers to whom all children have only their Christian names. He had wondered later if she had mistaken his first name for his last, or perhaps just didn't recognize any doctor except the kind that could do humankind some good. Whatever it was—and he was sure he knew—he had felt some nameless, profound emotion at the recognition he had heard in her voice.

He felt the same about this old lady. He was, of course, unable to tell her how life was. He had answered out of habit, "Just fine, thank you." That was what one said to a little old lady in a blue dress and pearls at Sunday dinner—not "one damn thing after another" or "hard at best" or "boring."

"Just fine, thank you," he had said as automatically as the janitor at school who always answered in the morning—whatever the question, or even if it were not a question at all but "Good morning" or "Hello, William." He always chimed out, "Jes' fine."

Miss Shoemaker had been a schoolteacher and had served as a missionary. After her opening sally, she wanted to know all about him, as if she were briefing herself for an evangelistic assault. He found himself talking freely, grateful for the fact that he was sitting at the end of the table and that the woman under the gyrating red poppy was jamming the airways so that only his nearest neighbor could hear him. Mr. Stroud, he thought, was trying to pick him up but couldn't quite get through.

"Oklahoma," Miss Shoemaker had repeated. "I always think of windmills and clean open spaces when I think of Oklahoma. Is it like that?" She had been to Africa but never to Oklahoma.

"Yes," he said in the kidding tone he sometimes took with old people, "windmills, but we don't joust with them."

He looked at her sideways, but she was very quick, "Oh, you should," she said. And then without stopping or looking at him, went on.

"Do you know, when I was a child, I thought that Don Quixote was the name of the donkey that Sancho rode? 'Donkey Hote,' " and he laughed as she chuckled, or at least shook a little more than usual. He liked her, and it surprised him that he found her so interesting.

He could almost hear his colleague in psychology at that party last fall, analytic and pedantic as ever, talking about how single people tended to relate not to peers but to elder persons.

"The single person continues the pattern learned in childhood, looking up to elder persons as the primary relationship. That accounts, more than fixation on grandparents, for the gravitation of unmarried persons toward the elderly."

That might be. Whatever the reason, Scriber was aware as he talked with Miss Shoemaker that he had been missing something in Collegemont where the elderly were an anomaly.

He continued eating, his mind wandering. Miss Shoemaker remained silent. She seemed to have a good appetite, though she took small portions from the bowls and platters that were passed around. She put down her fork and leaned toward him, saying in a kind of whisper, "Twelve."

He looked at his watch.

"One twenty," he said.

She looked around the table, "No, twelve people, twelve people at the table."

"Oh, right," he said, "I haven't eaten family style in a long time."

She drank some water. She had had a little of everything, and was eyeing the peach cobbler to which Mr. Stroud was helping himself. She held out a wicker bread basket to him:

"Will you have some more?"

He took a roll and as he silently ate, she sat sipping water until eventually the peach cobbler made its way around to them. They found that their portions were to be considerably smaller than those of Mr. Stroud or the teenage boy now bent over his plate. Miss Shoemaker offered him the crusty dessert:

"The bottom crust is sometimes the best part."

"Yes," he answered, and scraped the dish as he served them both.

He walked her to the "Dorcas," a narrow house on a side street.

"We have only breakfast here," she explained as they turned in to a walk bordered with the bearded iris his grandmother called blue flags.

"I would ask you in, but I always take a nap after lunch."

"So do I," he said, as he opened the screen door and then stepped back on the porch.

"Enjoy life," she said, "and your nap. We sit on the porch every evening almost."

It helped just to know that, he thought, as he said good-bye, and thanked her again for sharing lunch with him.

CHAPTER

26

Scriber walked back down Bethany Way. As he turned the corner toward the beach, he met the couple from the hotel, coming down the steps of their house.

"Hi," the girl said, "What lured you away from the beach?"

"Sunday dinner and a charming lady," he answered. He had started to add that you could count on Christians for good cooking, but he hesitated.

"Where did you eat?" the young man asked.

"At the big place down the block, with the blue canopy."

"Oh, in Beulah land, eh?"

Scriber was sure that it was an esoteric Biblical reference, but he didn't ask to be initiated. The man was carrying two rolled up towels.

"Going swimming?" Scriber asked.

"Yes, over at the Strand. We're going to change at the Inn."

They walked along together without agreeing to do so. Scriber asked if they knew a Miss Shoemaker who had been a missionary in Africa, but they didn't.

It seemed a good opportunity, so Scriber asked

the question that had been on his mind. "Why do you two spend the summer in a place like this, if you don't mind my asking?"

They were passing a completely deserted beach, and he read again the sign on the boardwalk, "Great Preaching by the Sea."

Mark looked at the girl and she seemed to give him a signal that he should do the talking.

"It's a kind of deprogramming," he said, glancing at Scriber as if he expected this question.

"Deprogramming," Scriber asked, "What's that?"

Mark was looking down, walking slowly with his hands in his pockets and the towels under one arm.

"It's like, you know, we are all programmed one way or another. The ad men and the politicians make a living because they know what turns us on, and it may even be that they make the decisions about what will turn us on; they decide on both stimulus and response."

He was becoming more animated.

"For example, do you know that the people in Detroit have big budgets for departments—called 'marketing research'—which try to figure us all out and to build cars which appeal to our drives and to our current anxieties? It's everywhere. We are constantly being programmed to buy things on cue. And of course, there are our parents and the schools, not as insidious as the ad men, but they do their part too. And all the while the good old church takes a hands-off attitude toward the things that really get to us—sex, for example—while these other guys are using it to sell cars and deodorant.

He stopped by the iron railing and the three of them

stood looking out to sea.

"Deprogramming means learning to respond to a new set of cues. And that's what you get here, if you want it, by hearing new words and living with people who are in some ways deprogrammed. Just look at this place. That empty beach on a Sunday afternoon says a lot. We're going swimming alright, but I know what the empty beach means. These people are trying to keep something worth keeping, the Lord's Day, for one thing, a day that is really different from all the commercialism and jazz that are eating up the earth and killing our spirits. And some of them are really against hedonism, the whole bit. But these people are more than quaint or world-hating. The old houses and clean ways, no neon or jazzy architecture; it all helps them to get back into another world, where words like "faith" and "salvation" and even "God" sound real. Even the Lord is for real. We come down here and tank up on that."

Ruthie had been silent but listening carefully.

"One day last fall," she said, "I got a letter from a friend, just an ordinary kind of hello-how-are-you kind of letter about things in general and nothing in particular. The letter ended with "God bless you." I sat there a long time—I was alone in my room—looking at that one word and repeating it to myself, then spelling it, G-O-D." She was speaking in a soft, almost reverent voice now. "The word had become strange to me, and I sat there just saying it over and over, and the more I did that, the stranger it sounded. It was like the opposite of what we usually do: we remember the person and forget the name. I remembered the name—it's always cropping up—but I couldn't shake the feeling that I was losing what it referred to. The way I was living, to use Mark's word, was programming me to not respond to my friend's words: 'God bless you.' It shook me up."

They were waiting for Scriber to speak.

"Is deprogramming a kind of brainwashing in reverse?" It seemed a lame question as he asked it. "It seems to me that you are saying that the way to keep your religion is to associate only with religious people. That could become a kind of ostrich-in-the-sand provincialism."

Mark knitted his brow, "Well, Jesus said that his disciples should be in the world but not of the world."

Scriber had heard the words many times since a time only dimly remembered now, when the football coach had met half a dozen boys in the church's damp basement to lead them through the Sunday school book and to hear their memory verses.

"Would you say that Sea Camp is in the world?" he asked.

"But that's just the point," Ruthie interjected. "It's harder for us not to be of the world than it was for his disciples. And Mark and I are not talking about whether people should swim on Sunday or smoke on the street and things like that. It's bigger. The disciples weren't bombarded by television and the slicks, and they didn't have so many distracting material things. We're really captive to our standard of living. That's the best thing about being here at the Camp, everything is simple, even the food, for example. And the rooms where we stay are the other extreme from the Holiday Inn."

"Speaking of which," Scriber said, "Could we walk in that direction? You are going to miss the sun, and I told a nice little old lady that I was going to take a nap. I am well programmed to that simple pleasure after Sunday dinner."

Walking back to the hotel, Scriber thought more about his companion at lunch. Miss Shoemaker, in saying goodbye on her front porch, had admonished Scriber to "enjoy life." That had come after their conversation which had begun with the question: "How's life, Scriber?" The old lady had not seemed at all nosey, or even unduly probing, just interested in him in a way he was not accustomed to. She seemed to sense that things were unsettled for the young professor, that he was on an unspoken quest, coping with some large, troubling question about the direction of his life. For a man just turning thirty, he seemed to be in conflict about that: now that I am no longer a boy, who am I and what am I going to do?

She had faced such a question when, as a middle-aged woman, she felt all the doors close after losing her beloved friend and companion, Helen, with whom she had lived happily for many years. The future seemed dark and she sought the counsel of her pastor. His gentle advice—to find a new vocation, one that used her skills as a teacher and suited her character—soon led to her work as a missionary teacher in Africa.

Later, as Scriber stretched out for a nap, Elaine Shoemaker's words, and her kind presence, stayed with him. "Enjoy life, Scriber."

CHAPTER

27

By 2 o'clock he was on the beach. He had no sooner spread his towel than Mark came striding toward him, in cut-offs and a white tee shirt.

"Hey, Scrib, have you tested the water yet?"

He placed his towel and took off his shirt and shorts to reveal a red Speedo. He sat close to Scriber, his knees drawn up and looking at the sea. His summer at the beach was evident, his body tanned and muscular, his hair bleached to a true blond.

Glad to have Mark's company, Scriber nonetheless asked where Ruthie was.

"Oh, she's got the afternoon shift today. I expect to see her for supper over at the Camp; she'll be singing in the choir this evening.

Just then a young man, vaguely familiar to Scriber, interrupted his jogging and walked toward them.

"Hi, Jerry!" Mark called out.

"Hey, Mark! So here you are." The boy squatted beside them as Mark said,

"This is Professor. . . "

Scriber quickly put out his hand. "Scriber. Good to meet you, Jerry.

"Good to meet you too, Scriber." Then to Mark: "Good party last night at the brown house. Good to see Todd and Gates. We missed you at Bible study this morning."

"Maybe next Saturday," said Mark, "If we are still here."

Jerry stood up. "Hope to see you soon, Mark. You guys have a good time on the beach."

As Jerry started jogging down the beach, Scriber recognized him as this morning's hitchhiker.

Mark stretched out on his side and looked at Scriber, "You're looking good after just a couple of days here."

Quite tan himself, Scriber's slight balding, slender form and hairy chest gave him a look both athletic and ascetic.

"Do you have the day off, Mark. By the way how old are you?"

"I'm 26. I'll check later to see if all is well at the Holiday Inn, but I'm free for the afternoon. You want to swim?"

"Sure, and since the surf is good, I might show you a game that I like to play. I wasn't very successful with two of my friends, Todd and Dorie."

The two men walked briskly into the waves, splashing themselves on chests and shoulders. When the water was about chest high, Scrib said: "If you would like to learn my game, this is about the right depth."

Mark stopped and looked quizzically at Scriber. "OK, what now?"

The waves were coming in steadily, as Scriber led the younger man out a little deeper.

"Now just stand in front of me, Mark, facing out to

sea, your feet on the bottom. When the next wave comes, just relax and let it bounce you off the sand. If it carries you to one side or another, just go with that. It's a kind of dance."

As Scriber stood behind Mark, holding his slender waist lightly, the wave lifted them both and they did a small pas de deux on and off the sandy bottom.

"That's it, Mark. Now here comes another wave. Just go with it, let the wave push you around."

Still holding his waist, Scriber guided the willing young man in the bouncing, lilting dance. Eventually he took a position beside Mark, and they continued to rise with each new wave, to feel their toes leave the sand and to drift lightly with the current, then find the bottom again. Mark seemed to get the rhythm of it. At one point he laid a hand on Scriber's shoulder as they danced together.

When they were again stretched out on the beach, Scriber suggested they get something cold to drink in his room.

He noticed as they entered the room that Mark had put out the "Do Not Disturb" sign and casually double locked the door. Scriber was getting out two Dr. Peppers. Mark had dropped his Speedo on the bathroom floor and was in the shower washing off the sand.

"You can dry your suit on the balcony, Mark," he said as he dropped his swimsuit and stepped into the shower, while Mark went out on to the balcony.

Both were now naked. Neither averted his eyes nor pretended not to notice the swelling of what was about to happen. Mark sat on the bed and patted a place for Scriber.

"Now," said Mark, "I'll teach you my game. Just lie

back, be easy, and close your eyes."

It was like nothing Scriber had ever experienced, Mark's hands and mouth all over his body, nothing said, everything becoming clear and clean, so much so that Scriber without a word was able to reciprocate, giving and receiving mutual joy. It was so exciting doing this for Mark, feeling his body tense and arch, then hearing his low deep voice groaning with pleasure.

They lay perfectly still for a while. Then as Scriber began to pull on white briefs, he asked, "Mark, would you like some dry shorts?"

"Sure. Thanks." Then with a sly, glancing smile, "I'll give them back next time."

They were sprawled on the cool sheets in their underwear, feeling the breeze and listening to the surf.

Mark yawned and stretched his arm, covering Scrib's face. Rolling over to face the older man, Mark asked, "I suppose you're wondering about Ruthie?"

"Yes, I have wondered about that. It looks to me like she is your girlfriend."

"Well she is, but friend is the big word there. She knows I'm gay. We met a few years back and have spent hours and hours just talking. Yes, she would have liked a relationship which included more than that, but she is my sweetheart in other ways. She is the one whose example I follow when it comes to living and acting sensibly. She even balances her checkbook. And she is on time for everything. Above all she has a smile for every occasion. You can imagine how helpful that was when I was having a lot of love/hate about myself.

"One day she asked me to her Bible study group. I

practically yelled, 'Your what!?' I've been down a lot of roads, but I never tried that one.

"Yes, my parents took me to church when I was a kid, but most of the family got over that. So I asked, Why? Ruthie explained that her group was made up of questioners and I might fit right in."

"So, yes, I went, and from the start the questions started flying. People actually laughed at the more crazy ones; I mean these people were having fun, in a serious sort of way. Before long I realized that the good humor laid the groundwork for exploring questions of faith. So of course I asked, What is faith? You may as well start from the beginning. And then, most remarkable to my ears, each person gave an account of why he or she believed in God or Jesus or whatever. It glued me to my seat. It was like a 12-step program, without the coffee.

"So I started attending and made some real friends there. Ruthie and I continued our conversations. She became aware that the underlying motivator or lack there of, for me, was being gay. She told me that just because I was free enough to be true to myself, that didn't mean that I could do whatever I liked. 'You're going to run off the rails, she said, 'if you party late, get up late and meet someone special TOO late. Time to grow up, boy. Why don't you talk to my pastor? He can be sort of like a shrink, but one who prays. I'll introduce him and when you see him, bring your baggage.'

"So I dutifully got in touch with him and we met on a Friday afternoon. It was not like what you see in the movies with someone listening behind a screen. There was no 'Father forgive me for I have sinned.' In fact this kindly man

155

sat facing me and he was in no mood to judge me or set up his own agenda. He only wanted to provide room for me to feel safe. I just sat there while he asked the loaded question.

'OK, Mark, tell me about yourself? Something is hurting you.'

"And so I just told him. I'm gay.

"He thoughtfully stared at me and I told him again. I'm gay. I've tried, but I just can't make myself any different. The real problem is that I can't seem to get out of this rut of casual party sex which I feel is getting in the way of what I would call my real, or ideal life. I drink and run around at all hours and show up late for work. My boss is patient, but I can see that he would like me to do better. My friends say that I have lost weight, and I don't feel as good as usual. I used to attend a church, where my mother was a nominal member. As close as I get to that now is your Bible study group, where Ruthie got me connected."

"I'm sorry, Mark," the pastor said, "that you are going through this and I will try and help. For starters, why would you say you are gay, if you are? Were you born gay, for example? Do you remember the first time you were attracted to men?"

"It was early on, no later than Mr. Bennett, my sixth grade teacher, sitting close at a concert he took me to. Never any girlfriends at all, and quite a lot of resentment toward my aunt, who kept pushing in that direction."

"So, would you say you have always been gay, that you were born that way?" "Yes, definitely yes." "So does that mean that God created you gay?" "Yes, I guess so."

"So, Mark," after a long pause, "wouldn't you say that

if God made you who you are, limping along with what you see at this time in your life as a wooden leg, don't you think that you are going to have to learn to dance with it?"

Silence filled the room, Mark recalled, as he thought about that. After some time he realized something may have shifted in him and it was worth seeing Pastor Phillips again. He planned on going back.

"God bless you, Mark. I'm glad to know that Ruthie is such a helpful friend. I look forward to picking up this conversation again. Now shall we pray?"

" Sure, Ok."

"Dear Father, our creator and redeemer and helper, bless Mark and help him to love himself as you so dearly love him. Strengthen him in every good purpose and show him your grace each day. Through Jesus Christ our Savior. Amen." "Thanks, Pastor Phillips," I said, "I have some things to think about."

Mark looked carefully at Scriber, wondering if he had said enough.

"That's OK, Mark. Go on. So you and Ruthie made your way down here after graduation from college and found jobs for the summer. And now you live at the Camp, just friends, as they say."

"Yes, that's the way people put it, but," Mark went on, "I would call it best of friends. She has helped me to drink less, to flirt less and to be more discriminating—that would be you!—to do a better job where I work, even to study the Bible and go to church here at Sea Camp. Most Sundays we have dinner at the Camp, very nice. I would say that after a year of knowing each other, we are real pals, open and honest, sharing a spiritual journey."

Scriber put on some fresh chinos and a polo shirt, while Mark got into his old cut-offs, over his new briefs.

Mark went on. "It has been Ruthie's friendship and that short time with Pastor Phillips, along with the Bible study group, that have been a big help in finding my way. In most ways, the church was never very helpful, in some cases downright hurtful.

"For awhile, when I was a teen, I went to my mother's church. The pastors were always quoting verses from the Bible that laid it out there: homosexuals were sinners because Leviticus and Romans said so, no two ways about it. The whole congregation seemed to agree, and any gay person in that church had to do a constant and clever job of hiding.

"My mother wasn't so quick to quote the Bible—which made her somewhat more tolerant—but she tended to agree with the sermons."

Scriber interjected, "You're right, the church I grew up in couldn't even conceive of dealing with homosexuality from the pulpit. Too far out. It seems to be a modern problem."

"Yeah," said Mark. "I guess I was born just in time to be caught in the middle. I got out of there as fast as I could, but as they say, you can run but you can't hide.

"Recently, this older couple, from that church, who had been very kind and generous to me, wrote me a letter. I had been home for my birthday and Christmas, with my room-mate. What happened during that visit, I can't say for sure. Though we had never discussed it, I believe that my mother had figured me out and that she knew what it meant that Jeff and I had been roommates for two years. I can imagine that

Dot and Oscar, my good friends when I was at the church, made some comment about my friend Jeff being home with me for a second Christmas. 'Oh,' my mother may have said, 'Jeff is much more than Mark's friend. It worries me, but he is my son.' Or something as revealing as that. "She probably presumed that they knew me better than they did, given their generosity to me in my high school years and now through 3 1/2 years of college. They had opened their home—their library, garden, and music collection to me. After I went away to college, Dot every Christmas picked apricots from their orchard and sent me a dozen of those little Gerber jars filled with her delicious apricot jam.

"Though I did not do so, I was confident that if I had asked them, this wealthy couple would have given me whatever I needed, all the more so as I was considering going to graduate school. I loved Dot and Oscar and they loved me. We often sat together in church, and took excursions in their big Packard. But then, early in the new year came the letter, typed and formal. I've shown it to Ruthie, and I have been carrying it in my wallet. Here, I'd like you to read it."

Dear Mark,

For almost two months we have tried to write this letter to you. It causes us extreme pain to write this as we must. It is so difficult to try to tell you how we feel.

When we were told of the perverted life you are living, we were physically ill. It was so hard to believe. Even now we often find ourselves trying earnestly to convince ourselves that it just cannot be true.

As you read your Bible, surely you are convicted of sin in

159

its ugliest form. Both the Old and New Testaments treat homo-sexuality with deep abhorrence, so in no way can we understand how a well-educated man can indulge in such sinful perversion.

We have prayed often that you will repent and turn com-pletely away from this sin. We want to help you in any way we can. If your problem is of genetic origin, you will have to over-come it by prayer and effort. But it can be done.

So if you come to see us to present your side of the story, we will listen but will never endorse it. We will always love you in the Lord, but can never have the same love for you that we had before this sad truth.

Love and prayers,
Dot and Oscar

"This is an example, Scrib, of the confusing conditional love which I experienced in the church. So maybe you can see how Ruthie's friendship has been like a hot-air balloon, lifting me quietly to a new place and a new view of the world and my possibilities."

Scriber stood up and wrapped his arms around Mark, smelling the soapy fragrance of his body—kissing the young-er man's neck: "Thanks, Mark, I want to see you again."

"Me, too," said Mark. "So, I guess I'll go check with the manager to see if anything has busted this afternoon."

"Oh, yes, Mark" said Scriber, "quite a lot has busted loose here this afternoon!" A hug, and Mark was off.

Scriber was finally relaxed, but still deep in thought, as he sat out on the balcony, listening to the surf and mulling over the day. Who could know how it would go with Mark, but whatever might develop, he would never be the same af-ter an unforgettable two hours.

CHAPTER

28

Just after four o'clock the telephone interrupted his dozing reverie. It was Dorie.

"We're in the lobby, Scriber," she said, but the voice could have been from the moon. He was groggy after the afternoon's activities and a half nap.

"Sure, come on up. 306."

Mr. Foyler put out his hand as they entered the room. "Good to see you, Scriber. I can see we woke you up. I like a nap myself on Sunday. That's the only day I can get one in."

The young professor shook hands with Mrs. Foyler, and then sat down beside Dorie.

"Have you had lunch?" he asked her, speaking close to her ear.

"Yes," she said, looking closely at him, "we ate at the College Inn after church. What about you?"

"Well," he said, baiting her, "I had lunch with a beautiful lady from faraway places who is spending the whole summer at the beach." He paused until everyone was looking at him. "She was a missionary in Africa and is eighty-five years old."

Mr. Foyler liked the joke, and his wife smiled as

broadly as she ever did. Dorie poked him in the ribs.

Mr. Foyler looked at his watch.

"We've got a two-hour drive, and if you two are going to the beach at all, you'd better go. You're driving back tonight?"

"Yes," Scriber said.

Dorie's mother said, "Pretty extravagant, young man, keeping your room in the afternoon." She had a way of interrogating without asking any direct questions.

"The nap was worth it," he answered, and then added, "You won't stay and have dinner? There are some quaint old boarding houses where they serve family style." He knew that they would want to be home before dark.

"Let's have a last look at the beach," said Mr. Foyler. The two wet swimsuits were hanging on a chair, the red Speedo not to be missed. They momentarily forgot about looking at the beach.

"You had company already?" asked Dorie.

"Oh, that belongs to a guy who works here at the motel. Nice guy from the foothills," explained Scriber.

Mrs. Foyler added, "Oh, that's good, that you have a friend here."

Mr. Foyler was silent, as Mrs. Foyler went on. "You know the old saying; if you leave something behind, it means you want to come back."

"Well," said Scriber, "he is the maintenance man here and gets only Sunday afternoons off."

They walked out to the car. Dorie kissed her father and then leaned through the car window to say goodbye to her mother. Scriber had kissed Mrs. Foyler once or twice, but he soon perceived that she enjoyed that no more than he liked the dry sensation of kissing a powdered cheek. So he just stood beside Dorie and thanked them again for bringing her down.

"Don't get too tired," Mrs. Foyler said to Dorie, "and drive home carefully. We'll see you later in the summer. I'll give you some jam then. And some for Scriber, too. Bye-bye."

And then they went to his room, Dorie giving him a rather full account of twenty-four hours with her parents.

"They've learned to keep a little more distance at last. You know, I think they are almost convinced that I am grown up."

"So am I," he said. "You'll have to be careful here."

"Of what," she asked, "of you?"

"No, of being deprogrammed."

"What's that?"

"Tell you later. Let's go swimming."

She went into the bathroom and closed the door. When she came out, she had on a one-piece pink swimsuit that accented just the spot where her waist was smallest. She was carrying a white swim cap, her hair falling down long and abundant.

He stood up from the bed where he had been sitting after having undressed and hurried into his swimsuit as if network television were going to pick him up any minute.

"Scrib," she said, standing close to him, "What is that on the mirror written in shaving lather?"

He had forgotten about it. "Oh, I was just fooling around. It was some interesting graffiti I saw on the way down here. I was just trying to punctuate it. You can read it several ways. Come on, that beautiful beach is waiting."

She did not move immediately. "The first word looked like 'Jesus,' " she said.

"That's right. Let's go."

They found a place down the beach from the motel in full view of the boardwalk and the amusement park. Scriber spread the blanket that he kept in his car and they sat down to watch the breakers.

"Before or after, what do you think?" He was flexing his biceps and showing Dorie the back of a lean brown shoulder.

She looked puzzled.

"Didn't you ever see those Charles Atlas ads for his body-building business? Some skinny guy would walk down the beach, and all the girls would titter. Then this big hunky man would come along and kick sand in the skinny fellow's face. That was 'before.' The 'after' showed the skinny guy with biceps like cantaloupes, and all the girls following him around with the big guy cowering in the background."

Dorie felt his arm. "Definitely 'after,' " she said. "Are you too muscle-bound, Charlie, to try the water, or do you just want to sit here and let all the passing cantaloupes compete for your body?"

"Let's swim, honeydew," he said pulling her toward the water.

Dorie was a strong swimmer. He followed her out beyond the breakers and they swam parallel to the beach, slowly making their way toward shore, going through all the strokes they knew. When Dorie did her version of the breaststroke,

Scriber could see how slim her waist was when she arched her back and then gulped air with a little gasping sound. Then she would roll on her back and kick and pull through the water with the perfect coordination of one of those water bugs that he used to watch skimming around the boat as he and his grandfather sat perfectly still watching two cork bobbers. Dorie would then roll over on her side and they would swim along face to face, and he could see her wet hair, too much of it for the cap, lying flat against her cheek, and her small feet working quickly with a motion that only a woman could make. The pink suit complemented her shimmering nut-brown skin, and her long lashes did funny things when her hazel eyes opened after each face-down stroke.

As they walked out of the surf, bracing themselves against the undertow of each receding wave, she pulled off her cap and her hair fell down on her shoulders, which he noticed, for the first time, were freckled.

"Have you been to the auction?" she asked. They had come ashore in front of the marquee, dark today, which announced TRASH AND TREASURE, 7:30 PM.

"No, but we can go if you like."

They walked along slowly, in silence, and Scriber knew that people were looking at them. He felt, as he often did when with Dorie, the sweet delight of possessing a beautiful thing and being envied for it. It wasn't that he wanted to be with Dorie only to parade her. But he did not refuse to savor the pleasure of being envied by others on the beach. He had been almost thirty years old before he really knew what such invidious comparison was, and the first time he had felt it, he began to understand why men go to war, and even why teenagers spend Saturday washing and waxing cars and Saturday nights driving up and down Main Street, one arm out the window and the other around a girl who has spent the day in rollers and relished anxiety. He had sometimes thought that the forty-dollars-a-couple restaurants would soon go out of business were it not for the possessive joy of male prowess that he was feeling now as he and Dorie strolled the beach. Charles Atlas had made a fortune on this moment, though the muscle-bound look seemed no longer in vogue, any more than women would long tolerate being worn like a man's adornment. But the moment was sweet to Scriber.

They lay on their stomachs, Dorie with her eyes closed. He touched her shoulder, making small circles as if playing in the sand. "I used to have freckles," he said.

She opened her eyes: "You still do."

"I mean I really had freckles. You couldn't see me for the freckles. My favorite aunt knew that I didn't like them, and she used to say, 'Freckled boy, handsome man.' And my grandfather said he'd never known a freckle-face who wasn't smart. But I really worried about those freckles. I even held half a lemon on my nose once because I overheard some girls at school talking about that. Good thing it didn't work. I would have looked pretty funny with a bleached nose. Your freckles are nice." He pretended to count them on her nose.

She propped herself up, her chin in both hands. "Do you remember the auction we went to, Scrib? The one out in the country where you bought that milking stool?"

She didn't have to wait for him to say that he remembered. "That was the best one we've been to. I had no idea that we would stay there all day."

He remembered it as well as she did, and he had thought of it many times since the summer day when they had driven out of Collegemont on the patched concrete highway where a new brick sign announced that Sherwood Forest Estates would soon be built. Beyond where the dirt road left the gravel, a knot of cars identified the place. They left their car to gather red dust with the others and walked up the road.

A red-lettered poster—like the ones showing his grandfather's picture that they used to tack up on telephone poles, or like the ones they used to put up in barber shops to announce revival meetings in Lincoln—announced the AUCTION, at which the Jackson Brothers would sell all the worldly goods of Miss Maggie Williams.

The lane that led up to the house was showing signs of neglect. They walked, Dorie in one rut and he in the other, past the falling-down barn, up to Maggie Williams's house, as innocent of paint and about as old as the oak tree whose roots surfaced at its front door. The house was more of a cabin with a porch on the front; the roof came down so low that tall men had to stoop. The cabin had been emptied, and unpainted tables and chairs and beds, old quilts, jars, churns and tools, a well bucket—everything people once needed to live— littered the porch and the yard under the tree.

People were poking through everything while the auctioneers, looking like little preachers in white shirts and ties and felt hats, stepped up on the packing crate and spoke into the mike, interrupting the bluegrass music with "testing one, two, three, four." One of those hot sandwich trucks that looked quilted pulled up, and the crowd began to settle down for the day.

"Do you remember that the first thing they sold was a cracked old jug and it brought $23? I knew right then that I had not brought enough money to compete with nostalgia."

"Or to pay for your own," Dorie said as she dribbled a handful of sand on his back. "We spent a whole Saturday out there," she went on, "in the sticks. And when the gal in the checkered pants and orange shirt covered the Jackson boys' lunch break with gospel music, I was sure you would want to leave." There was irony in Dorie's voice. "Do you remember she sang, something like 'Jesus and me,' or was it 'Me and Jesus'?"

"She was definitely 'after'," Scriber said, "and more like watermelons."

They had in fact spent the day sitting on the roots of the old tree, watching the past go by in rub-boards and iron wash tubs, crocks and wind-up telephones, medicine bottles and pots and a cradle. The auctioneers had been evangelistic about it. They knew the old language. Scriber hadn't heard the word "asfiditide (as-fid- i-teed)—he had looked it up in the dictionary when they got home that day and learned that it was actually "asafetida"(asa-fe-teeda) —since his mother had talked about how her mother had put this exotic spice in a pouch around the children's necks to ward off colds at school.

When one of the Jackson brothers went out into the crowd and put his arm around the shoulders of a shy woman to help her bid, Scriber had felt something which he could not identify as either homesickness or revulsion—both surfaced.

But there was no doubt in his mind that what he had felt had less to do with where he was that day than where he had been as a teenage boy in Oklahoma where he had witnessed this very same scene: loud, aggressive men, mixing sex and social pressure and nameless loves and fears to move people out of pews and down to the front, where a sympathetic preacher was waiting to kneel and pray. In more formal and liturgical churches it would have been an invitation to receive such tangible and homely and unassuming gifts as bread and grape juice perhaps, in little skinny glasses.

He had bought not only the milking stool but some oak chairs that he hoped to restring himself.

They had driven back to town in the late afternoon, Scriber feeling as good as if they had spent the day at his grandparents' farm.

Just before they reached the paved road, Dorie had said, pointing to the idle bulldozer at the edge of the woods, "How long do you suppose it will take to clear the trees so they can build Sherwood Forest?"

"More trash than treasure, I'll bet," responded Scriber when Dorie, still lying on her stomach and looking toward the boardwalk, commented, "What people will pay for something that reminds them of the past! Just, for example, what are you going to do with that milking stool?"

"Why, Dorie, you could stitch a fancy needlepoint cushion for it, maybe cats or a house with smoke coming out of the chimney. That would be a good project for those winter nights when you sit home and rock by the warmth of color television." He paused. "Or maybe I'll get a cow, I've always had a weakness for cows."

She looked sideways at him, amused.

"Do you know," he went on, "that cows know when it is going to rain? They lie down and save themselves a dry spot. The first thing our own Bill Meteor, our weatherman, does every morning on the way to the studio is to drive past the pasture by the airport and see how many of the cows are lying down. Three cows out of ten lying down, thirty percent chance of rain." She giggled.

"Do you realize, dear Dorie, how many things cows do for you? Milk, butter, cheese, ice cream; not to mention leather and pastoral landscapes, fuel for the Indians to cook their curry and floor wax for the Africans. And now the noble bovine has gone into meteorology. And you ask me what I will do with a milking stool? I may just keep it in the living room, quite unadorned, to remind me of all those nameless cows standing and lying in green pastures, quietly chewing, making milk and mooing peacefully, and now and then casting a keen long-lashed eye at the sky so that you and I will know whether or not to carry an umbrella. Why the more I think of it, the more that milking stool looks like a place to sit and contemplate the sheer gift, the immeasurable abundance of the great creator. Why, there are even cows on the tower of the splendid cathedral at Laon. Who says only Hindus appreciate the fulsome cow?"

Dorie turned on her side, facing him. "What do you mean, floor wax for the Africans?"

"They use the aromatic dung of the cow on the dirt floors of their rondavels. It creates a hard, smooth surface and makes the whole hut smell sweet. They sweep their houses every day, clean as a pin, though they wouldn't come across very well on a television commercial or in *Better Homes and Gardens*, except for maybe the garden section. Let's see, what would the ad men call it? How about, 'Green Sheen, the organic floor wax,' or 'Nature-Glo, a Touch of the Out-of-Doors.'"

Dorie put one finger under the waist-band of his trunks, pulled and let it pop against his side.

"Maybe I will make you a needlepoint cushion," she said, "featuring a cow. Do you want to swim some more?"

He got up on his hands and toes like a man about to do pushups and sprang quickly to his feet. He pulled her up by both hands and they ran toward the water.

"Oh, I was in the sun too long. It feels cold," she said, standing just to her knees in the surf. A large wave broke and she retreated. But the white water caught her and she might have been bowled over had Scriber not caught her around the waist. He pulled her hard against himself and then, turning his back to the breakers, half swam, half walked backward toward deeper water. A wave began to break behind and above them. He bent his knees against Dorie's and both of them ducked under the crest. Dorie came up sputtering, and Scriber, his arm still around her waist, swam backward as they both kicked, almost in sequence.

Her hands were on his chest, and they bounced gently on the bottom and rose as easily with the next wave. He held her now at arm's length, and as one wave after another came, they rose with it and then fell to dance lightly on the sand in the swell's gentle decline. Once they went simultaneously all the way to the bottom, their extended legs side by side, and it seemed to Scriber that her pink swimsuit turned the color of rosé wine in the play of light and water as they touched the sand and then floated, coming closer together, to the surface.

Dorie pulled away playfully and began to swim on her back out to deeper water. He did not follow her immediately but treaded water as she disappeared under a wave, her small feet kicking against the sky. She had played the game with him, as much as a person could play it with another. He wasn't sure that she even knew what had happened, that for six or seven waves they had done it together. He put his head down and began to swim strongly toward Dorie who was waving to him.

They spent the fading afternoon on the beach. She slept awhile and woke up to find Scriber sitting in the position of a yogi, watching her sleep. The couple from the motel had come strolling down the beach, and Scriber had introduced Dorie. They mentioned that there would be a service at the tabernacle at 7:30, and after they had gone on down the beach, Scriber had tried to explain what the Camp was and how he had come to meet Mark and Ruth.

"It's sort of like Maggie Williams's auction," he had suggested, feeling strangely embarrassed to talk about it with Dorie and a little resentful that it had intruded upon this particular afternoon.

"Trash and treasure, you mean?" she said half seriously.

"I think you may have hit on it," he said. "Are you hungry?"

The first lights were coming on along the boardwalk as they walked to the motel, though the sun had not yet set. Scriber, still in his swimsuit, sat on the balcony while Dorie showered.

The few clouds above the dark sea were beginning to turn the color of a young girl's cheeks, and from far down the beach he could hear the carrousel. He lost track of time; he went inside to get his watch.

The room was dark. He found his watch among the coins and keys on the dresser and was reaching toward the lamp when the bathroom door opened just wide enough to send a shaft of light into the room. Scriber did not move until Dorie called:

"Scrib, will you please hand me that little white case?" The volume with which she spoke told him that she thought he was not in the room.

"Sure," he called out. He found the case by the foot of the bed and tapped the door wide enough to reach a hand and forearm around it. Scriber saw her in the steamy mirror, in the translucent pinkness he had seen when they sat on the sea's floor an hour earlier. It was not that he had tried to play the peeping Tom, or that he had tried not to. He had just seen that what was there was of that same quality.

When he had gone into the bathroom later, still salty and carrying a pair of jeans, neither Dorie nor her steamy shower had erased the graffiti. He reached out one finger and moving his lips, shaped the words slowly: "Jesus want make you love." He added no commas, and rubbing his finger in the wet soap that Dorie had left, he underscored the last word.

CHAPTER

29

It was seven o'clock when they reached the Beulah. He knew that Dorie had probably never seen a real boarding house, so they had decided, at his suggestion, to go over there for supper. A young woman in a gingham apron was just putting a rope across the dining room door as they walked in.

"Hurry," she said, "we have food left, but everyone has to finish by 7:30."

Sunday evening supper was a buffet of chicken and ham, and vegetables that were more than likely warmed over from lunch. The woman who stood behind the table could have been anyone's favorite aunt, large-boned on a scale with her generous servings, smiling over the steaming trays.

"You two just find a table, and when you are ready, I'll bring you some homemade ice cream. There's plenty left."

Scriber and Dorie sat down, their plates full, at one of the long tables just as four ladies were leaving. One of them said, as she moved sideways out of her chair and then stood up stiffly but finally straight, "Remember, the song service starts at 7:30, so don't you young people be late."

They ate quickly, hungry as they were, and the ice cream was as good and large-grained as if he had been taking turns with his father and grandfather cranking it and then packing it in burlap sacks and lots of salt and sitting around for an hour that seemed like two until his mother came out with bowls and a big spoon. They ate every bit of it.

When they came out of the front door of the Beulah, Scriber suggested that they sit and rock for awhile. On almost any other day he would have wanted to get in the car and start home. But the car was a mile away, as many cars were, and besides, this day had been, to say the least, remarkable, one to frame and keep. He was in no mood for hurrying, or for losing what today augured for his future relationship with Dorie.

"Let's sit on the porch and watch the night come," he said, as he pulled a rocker for Dorie closer to the one he had chosen for himself. After agreeing that it had been a good dinner, neither spoke for some time. Scriber noticed after awhile that they were rocking in rhythm.

People in casual summer clothes had been going by in a steady stream, and Dorie seemed fascinated by the sight. Some spoke in low tones, but many walked in silence, which was broken after a few minutes by the bells which Scriber had heard on the beach that morning. He knew the tune, and he began to rock in time with the music; it seemed to him that Dorie too was moving to the slow melody. Fewer people were passing now, and the lady who had served them ice cream went sideways down the stairs and turned with short, quick steps toward the sound of the bells.

"Would you like to go, Scrib, since we are here?" He would have been content just to sit there and enjoy the deserted place, to hear the bells at a distance. But he could see that she was curious.

"Why not?" he said, "but it may be more trash than treasure." As if to differentiate himself from the procession toward the desultory bells and the glowing cross, he pointed out to Dorie, in the detached tone of a tour guide, the big lodges and the canvas houses. They stopped to read the inscription on the statue that stood between the fountain and the gazebo: "He who comes to me shall not thirst."

Even after they were inside, Scriber felt the need to objectify the experience by commenting on it. He was always annoyed with people who talk during a play, even at the movies, or who felt it necessary on an early morning walk or while playing tennis to keep up a conversation. He had observed that people often were driven to compulsive talking at precisely the wrong time: after a long separation, in the face of grief, even during sex. He knew what it was to feel someone trying to engage him and to resist that pressure, as he or she works to gain control by reducing the threatening new experience to familiar words.

Perhaps that is what inevitably happened to religious experience when awe in the face of wonder at life's mystery became ritualized and institutionalized. Then the experience behind the paraphernalia gets lost, and religion becomes words about the experience so that if you had the words, you could think that you had the experience. Like a would-be lover who senses that what he feels could get out of hand, Scriber tried to stay at a safe distance from what was happening around him.

"Look at that ceiling, Dorie," he said, craning his neck. "There must be an acre of golden oak in that. And that explains the acoustics in this place."

About half of the seven or eight thousand seats were taken, and people continued to come in as the organ's opening notes vibrated like the big tub of an organ at Radio City. Several men in dark suits, carrying books, came in from some hidden place and sat down in tall chairs behind a dozen baskets of gladioli. A younger man in a peppermint-stick coat appeared from another secret place and, standing behind the big pulpit which was, Scriber noticed, also of golden oak, encouraged them all to join in singing. Little encouragement was needed. The organ could do everything but make it rain, and the man playing it enjoyed his work. There were no hymnbooks for the opening "song fest," and when Scriber leaned over to Dorie to say that this was better than artillery punch, he could not hear his own voice.

It was, more or less, what he expected. He had seen most of it before, though not on this scale, in the summers out in Oklahoma and even occasionally on regular Sundays when the minister seemed to have spotted some lost sheep among his flock, or when he got the notion that a good many of his flock were in fact lost sheep, or goats. At college during Religious Emphasis Week there had been live testimonials such as the tall young man was giving now. Scriber had noticed him right away, sitting with a young woman behind the second basket of gladioli. When he stood up to walk to the pulpit, he looked out of place up there in his tennis tan, blazer with wide lapels, and academic mien.

It turned out he had just graduated from college and was going to graduate school in urban planning. His family, as he said, had been coming to the Camp for three generations —"the beach is not bad"—and he believed that it had been

177

providential for him to be there for ten or twelve summers. He had been led both to urban studies and to his fiancee (to whom he once unwittingly referred to as "my wife" toward the end of his talk). So far as Scriber could make out, everything that had happened to him thus far was Providence. When he sat down, he got some scattered "amens" from the congregation and a quick little kiss behind the gladiola from the girl with shiny hair.

A large choir of young people sang "The Battle Hymn of the Republic" and then a regiment of men in dark suits, and carnations, came in lock step to take up the collection. Scriber put a dollar bill in the straw basket. Then a woman who appeared to be an aging refugee from the Metropolitan Opera sang something of which neither he nor Dorie could understand one word.

He occupied himself during the solo studying the ribbon-like sign, like the one around that wedge-shaped building in Times Square (except that this one was stationary) which spanned the front of the auditorium in letters four feet high: I AM HOLY SO BE YE HOLY. Scriber half hoped that the preacher—who must be the young man in the tallest chair— would comment on that. He couldn't remember not knowing the phrase, but he had no clear idea of what it meant. He had never once thought to ask why the Bible always featured it in gold lettering, and he had little curiosity about the hymn they used to sing every other Sunday, which started by repeating this admonition three times. He thought maybe I AM HOLY meant that the Lord did not want people on his beach on Sunday, and that BE YE HOLY had special significance for the man in a black suit, white shirt and narrow dark tie, who peeked from between the sixth and seventh baskets of gladiola wearing the expression of someone who had been weaned on lemons.

He also seemed quite unmoved by the gala moment in the service when, just before the sermon began, a large neon flag above the choir rippled red, white, and blue, its stars twinkling in electronic sequence, as the congregation stood to sing 'My Country, 'Tis of Thee."

The preacher, introduced as Chris Matick, was obviously the man of the hour. Three chimes sounded and the people all knew to bow their heads. It was as quiet as any place he had been since his last camping trip to the mountains.

The preacher was standing spotlit in the pulpit. He was not much older than Scriber and, for that reason alone, stood out among the ministers on the platform. He too wore a dark suit, but the cut was continental, like Scriber's new Italian jacket. He stood perfectly still, as if he were not in the spotlight. He had the lean face that Scriber always associated with discipline, and his neatly cut dark hair added to his generally ascetic appearance.

He turned several pages in the large Bible and said simply, in a voice that was both soft and clear: "Tonight I want to talk with you about this text, from an obscure parable of Jesus: 'Every scribe who has been trained for the kingdom of heaven is like a householder who brings out of his treasure what is new and what is old.'"

Scriber's ears perked up at the word 'Scribe' in the reading. He listened as the young preacher began his sermon by explaining that this was actually a little parable, a 'mini-parable.' He pictured a man who had many valuable things, some of them new, like a house, a new job, even a new style of life. And the man had old things too, things from his family—old friends, memories, tradition. Sometimes he loved the new things better than anything, and there were times when he craved the old. Often he would wake up in the middle of the night, or too early in the morning, thinking about all that he wanted to do, all that he had to do. And sometimes, when he was under stress, trying to cope with too many things, when things weren't good at work, or at home, he would go into the bedroom and get out the old family quilt, which his grandmother had made by hand, and he would curl up under it on the bed, and the new, frightening world would go away, at least temporarily. Sometimes his wife and children, their home, were like that old quilt to him, and he resented their sharing their problems with him when he came home after a hard day. And sometimes, when the old memories—guilty memories out of the past, memories which sometimes did not even surface to consciousness—made him anxious with a nameless fear, he would work like a madman to buy new things. Or do new things, or just fill his every waking hour with one project after another. He used the new to escape the old, and the old to escape the new. But, said the preacher, there was a better way, a way of living as a whole person with both the old and the new.

Scriber was listening but not listening. The sermon became for him a collage of the preacher's words and his own, and he found himself running away from the sermon to the "black-eyed Susan" quilt that his grandmother had quilted stitch by stitch. It was his own life the minister described.

He would hasten to listen again, and then to look
secretly at Dorie, who listened as politely to this sermon as
she no doubt had to one that morning sitting in the Presbyterian church with her parents. Then drifting away again, to
his fetal retreat under the quilt; perhaps that was what this
whole thing was about. Maybe religion meant no more than
crawling under that quilt and feeling as secure as a farm boy
who has had a good supper and now lies deep in bed under
heavy covers listening to the cold rain beat on a tin roof not
three feet from his head, who falls asleep knowing that tomorrow he will wake to a warm kitchen and a hot breakfast
that will begin with the same prayer that has been said at that
table three times a day for his whole life. Maybe that is what
"Holy" means, under a quilt protected from the cold rain, or
smelling hot oatmeal in the dish under your nose while you
hear a prayer which you could easily repeat, having heard it
so many times. It is the woman who cooked you the oatmeal
who intones it, but even you, who comes here only on holidays to ride with your cousins and sleep with them up in the
attic, could say it.

Maybe the Lord is Holy because he is like a quilt who
keeps away the real world, a memorized prayer that works
like an incantation to keep at bay all that waits out there.
To change that prayer, to try to make it more reflective of
the changing world into which the woman was sending her
children, fed on oatmeal and country cream and cherishing
a mother with her forehead in her hand praying the same
prayer over every meal, to change that prayer would be to
destroy it. What would matter to these five boys and their
five sisters later on, even more than their good skin and teeth

derived from that wholesome food and those outdoor chores, would be not what the woman said but that she had said it, and that she had said it in a certain way. The words of the prayer were irrelevant as were the pieces of shirts and feed sacks and Sunday dresses in the old quilts that kept them warm.

It was the way it felt, the ritual that mattered. And that was precisely what was becoming clear to Scriber Newall as he sat listening to the preacher, perched astride the old ways of growing up and the social and intellectual relevance of Protestantism that had until recently given him something to do on Sunday morning.

It was all so predictable, that he should be here on a Sunday night in a nineteenth-century camp meeting next door to a carnival, and that even in the midst of it he should want to be here and not want to be here. That had been his story, from one extreme to the other: from the Oklahoma hills to the East, from that summer at church camp when he was about to decide for the ministry to his present embarrassment at all pious talk, from small-town boy to academic to whatever he was now.

The preacher had warmed up and was repeating his text. The question he asked began to dominate Scriber's collage.

"Now you've tried to find it back there somewhere in the way you want it to have been but it never was. Or you try to find it in the future that never turns out to be what you imagine. You haven't found it, have you? Where could it be? What could put it together, put you together? Where could you lose yourself and find yourself at the same time?

"Jesus said that that would happen in the kingdom of God where the old—forgiven, cleansed, lifted beyond mere memory to gratitude and compassion, for others and for yourself—and the new—where license gives way to freedom and every opportunity becomes a possibility for love—the old and the new come together where God forgives and makes you able to love your neighbor and your 'lover' and your enemy and yourself as well."

The preacher had caught fire and seemed to be standing on his tiptoes, not shouting, but speaking with such earnestness that Scriber was sure he spoke of himself, of some transformation in his own life.

"Jesus suggests in this parable that life is neither in the past nor the future, but that God is with us now, like an overpowering lover who holds us and moves so that all we have ever done is called good, or if not good in itself, then good for what it has taught us and for the moment to which it brought us. And all that is yet to be is full of joy and hope even though it may, like this moment, be full of pain and self-abandonment and risk. For all of this there is "plenty good room" in the infinite spaciousness of God that we call Salvation."

The preacher paused, but Scriber's mind raced ahead, or perhaps backwards, and he tried to make a place in his soul for God the Great Lover, to remember in his boyhood or some more recent time what was buried under his alternating cynicism and sentimentality. Even then the preacher was talking to him, the preacher was talking to him, and he was resenting it even as it was happening. He was like a prim woman protesting flirtation while wanting all the time to respond.

The sermon ended, and the house lights were going up and the organ started, so loud that it could surely have no higher place to go. The man in the peppermint-stick coat was motioning for them to stand up. The preacher and another minister came down and stood in front of the baskets of flowers, and by the time the hymn was over, some of the people had gone to the front to speak with them.

As they left by a side door, Dorie stifled a yawn: "It wasn't as much fun as the auction, was it?"

Scriber took her hand and pulled her with him as he almost danced, nimble as a boy getting out of school, down the steps. "I know what would be fun," he said. "Do you hear it?"

CHAPTER

30

The streets of Sea Camp were becoming deserted, as the congregation dispersed to the tent-houses and the big lodges. There were of course, no cars moving on the street. The streetlights were old and burned yellow, and in the front parlor of the Beulah, a leaded-glass lamp kept a dim and lonely vigil. The brightest light was behind and above them, and from that direction the last bells of that Sunday began, almost drowning out the distant sound of the carrousel.

"Camp meetings and carnivals," Dorie said, "you can sure pick 'em, Scriber Newall."

He put his hand over her shoulder and pointed through the window of the Goshen where a stained glass lamp burned red and green and yellow, and one bent figure sat among the bric-a- brac of an earlier time.

"Now I ask you, Dorie, is that a boarding house with one lady who stayed home to read her Bible, or is it the biggest bordello this side of Texas where the madam waits for all these lusty Christians, hotter than ever from all that singing and preaching?"

(In the 19th century camp meetings there was action in the bushes to match the histrionics of the revivalist gatherings. Quite a number of pregnancies followed the extended

185

retreats that could continue for as long as a month, not unlike the "camping out" of Sea Camp.)

He stopped though he could see that Dorie wanted to go.

"No, seriously, Dorie, can you tell for sure? Listen. Can you tell which is the organ and which the calliope? How much of this, do you think, is biology and how much theology? That young preacher for example. Would an old bald guy with a squeaky voice be as popular even if he could explain what that sign meant, the one about being holy. You can't separate them, this and the carnival. I wonder if that word has any connection with 'carnal!' "

He was talking as much to himself as to Dorie now. "Carnal camp and campy carnival, side by side, two of a kind. I'm not saying that that is bad. I'm just trying to understand what it really means, why they have that big sign up there, of all the words they could have chosen. Maybe they know how close what they are espousing is to sex and so they put up a reminder in letters five feet high, warning folks not to get carried away like the people in those camp meetings out in Kentucky or someplace where a good many of the young girls went home full of religion and even more than that. Here they even put up a fence and chain the beach on Sunday, and maybe that's part of the reason for keeping cars out of here. I don't know."

They had reached the boardwalk, and he could tell by Dorie's silence and the slow way they were walking that she didn't follow much of what he was saying, but she didn't mind his going on like this.

"I was wondering what my grandfather would make

of that, 'Be ye holy.' He and Nina, my grandmother, were lovers until they came with the ambulance and took him off to the hospital in Clearwater where he died. I remember the day. I had come up from college when he had the first attack. They slept together even when he was sick. And when they were taking him out of the house, the sheet pulled up just to his stomach (you could still see he had a good chest and everything), he said to her—not loud so that people would hear—'Do you reckon, Nina, they've got a bigger bed than this in that hospital?' It was just like him, and she knew what he meant and bent over right there and kissed him. He was sixty-seven, and he had married her when she was sixteen.

"I remember how he used to put on his blue-striped apron that she had made just for him, tall as he was. He stood there as they did the dishes, just because he liked to be with her, pinching and kissing her all the while. And when I think of that, I think I have seen it all. Anyway, I just wonder what 'Be ye holy' would mean to him. Sometimes I thought he only went to church so he could sit close to her, she was always so busy around the house. But there was something else in it too."

The pavilion that separated the Camp from the Strand was busy. They saw people from the tabernacle, some of them still carrying bibles, strolling up the boardwalk. It was obvious that they were enjoying the noise and color of so many Sabbath breakers. Holiness, like sin, Scriber thought, must be all the more delectable in a foreign environment, like being the only person with a tan at a party in the middle of February.

Dorie pulled him toward the arcade. She had spotted an astrological weighing machine, a fancy one that gave a horoscope along with one's weight, for a nickel. Dorie found two coins in her purse.

"My treat," she said, "you first."

He put the nickel in the slot marked Sagittarius. As soon as the needle reached 158, a small card appeared from a slot, like stamps from a machine. He read aloud: "Take advantage of new opportunities today, and strengthen old attachments. Take time for reflections before a new venture." He turned the card over. There was the archer, his bow drawn, and underneath was written: "Sagittarians are most often philosophers, theologians, or clowns."

Dorie's card told her that she should beware of new ventures today and consolidate her resources for a future opportunity. "Libra," the card said, "is the sign of free spirits." She laughed.

"For that nickel I am told how free I am but that the best thing I could do today would be to stay in bed and save my money."

"Never mind," he said, "I am going to take advantage of the opportunity to buy some peanuts, and you can both save your money and share that venture as well. Who knows, I may even strengthen my old attachments."

They found a bench just outside the pavilion and sat facing the carrousel, their hands occasionally meeting in the bag of peanuts between them.

They had no sooner sat down than Scriber heard Mark's voice. "Hey, Scrib, did you learn anything about the future? Hi, Dorie?"

A little surprised that he had remembered her name,

Scriber stood up: "Hi, Mark, hi, Ruthie. That's right, you met Dorie earlier at the beach. Have you had a good afternoon?"

"Yeah" said Mark. "I guess you'll be going home soon. Maybe it won't be too long before you come back. The beach is great later in the summer; the water warms up and the tourists drop off."

Dorie was quiet, then said to Ruthie, "Do you enjoy singing in that big choir?"

"Oh, yes, it's fun; a lot of enthusiasm, wouldn't you say?"

"No doubt about that," said Dorie. "You've probably made some good friends in the choir."

"Oh, yes. Aren't you glad that Scrib met a swimming buddy for his short visit here?"

Scriber added guardedly: "Yes, I'm glad to have met you too, Ruthie. Do you expect to work here and to live at the Camp beyond the summer?"

"I'm not sure, and I believe Mark's plans are not clear either. Is that right, Mark?"

"No, I mean, yes, that's right; not sure yet," Mark said, looking quickly but directly at Scriber, a move not to be missed by Dorie.

"Well, we are about to ride the merry-go-round," said Scriber, "It looks like fun."

"It is fun, said Mark. "I've had a big day, and I believe Ruthie has too; we're both working tomorrow."

"We'll be driving back to Collegemont. Really good to meet you, Ruthie, and to have a swim with you, Mark, I will leave your Speedo at the desk." They said good-byes all around and Ruthie and Mark walked on up the beach.

Scriber took up where he had left off.

"I remember visiting them a year or two before he died," Scriber said, as if he had not been interrupted. "He had just retired, but nothing seemed to have changed much, just that he was around more and my grandmother relaxed her rule about no naps on the beds during the day. She cooked all the things my grandfather and I liked, especially chicken and dumplings.

"We went to church on Sunday morning, which was a good place to see family and everyone else. I woke up that morning to a feather tickling my nose and the smell of my grandmother's cooking. They washed up after breakfast while I shined my shoes, and my grandfather's too, on the back porch where the separator sat. That morning as I turned the geared wheel that separated out the cream from what became skim milk, I could hear my grandmother splashing around in her Sunday morning bath.

The sun came in from the east windows which ran the whole length of the kitchen, and on its brightest mornings you couldn't have found a crumb or a piece of dust after she had washed and swept and worried over every lurking speck.

"My grandfather's striped apron must have been in the wash for Monday, or maybe he was just having fun. Anyway, he had on a pink and green flowered one made out of feed sacks. It was too short for him. When he had finished drying the dishes and she was trying to sweep, he did a little dance around the kitchen and asked her if she wouldn't rather dance with him than that old broom which got too much of her time. She swatted at him with the broom and said they were going to be·late and what a pretty apron he had and wasn't he a sight and to stop it because she had to put the roast in before we went to church.

"We were a little late, and it was beautiful, walking up to the church with the people already singing inside and the sun shining and my grandfather giving her his arm as we slowly climbed the steps. The choir, in wine-colored gowns and white collars, sang something unmusical but happy. A neighbor saw my grandfather and turned right around in the pew to shake his hand. The preacher gave a sermon about what hell would be like and how we ought to give up the world so as not to go there.

"I've forgotten most of it, but what I do remember is how little it had to do with that fine morning and those two people sitting close to each other beside me there. He pinched her knee as if to say about the fiery sermon, 'Now don't you worry, Nina.' My grandfather looked frequently at the new shine on his shoes. At the door he said to the sweating preacher, 'This boy is my grandson, who's come all the way up from college to see us.' If it hadn't been the preacher he would have called me 'peckerwood' or 'punkin'eater,' and showed the fine shine on his shoes."

Dorie had shelled a handful of peanuts and held them out to him in a closed fist.

"Have more peanuts, peckerwood. They will make you as sexy as your grandfather."

"He was sexy alright," Scriber said with his mouth full of peanuts, "and a lot more. Let's have that spin on the merry-go- round."

191

CHAPTER

31

Scriber bought two tickets from the caged woman who pushed them toward him as if she were selling subway tokens rather than a ride on two prancing, leaping horses between the lake and the sea. Though she did not speak, he said "Thank you," in the tone that someone might use to thank the server at a restaurant.

There was about Scriber that night the bearing of a small boy, and as he and Dorie got in line, he realized even before she echoed the word, that he had called the whirling amusement ride by a name he thought he had forgotten.

"Do you remember," Dorie was asking, "the first time you rode a merry-go-round?" She had paused at just the right place to dust off the word that he had, at some impulse as elusive and surprising as memory and dreams, brought down from the attic of his mind.

"Sure, the first one we had to push. I can see my father still, reaching out and catching a pole and coming round with it and then catching another. One day when my stomach turned over, he had caught a pole and pulled back hard, but not before I had given him a poor reward for his effort. Maybe that was when I began looking for a substitute for 'merry-go-round.' But don't worry, I don't get sick anymore, just when I read in a car."

He was speaking loudly to be heard above the calliope. The music, he knew, was loud enough to reach as far as the Holiday Inn, or even to that brown house at the end of the boardwalk. He had heard it even above the organ as they left the tabernacle. (He had been puzzling over why there had not been more of a call to come forward in response to what the preacher had said. Not that he would have done that, or even stayed for it, but he had expected it to happen.) Once they were outside he had heard it immediately—wild, sweet notes that seemed to cut through the organ.

Now, standing where they could feel the rush of wind from the flying horses and hear the little cries of delight, the music was so loud that Scriber could hardly hear his own voice and sometimes felt that he was talking to himself. He put his cupped hands to Dorie's ear, like someone telling a secret. "I've been hearing this for two days, now I'm going to ride it with you!"

Dorie turned and smiled at him, and there was in it a look which told him that she was seeing something she had not seen before, and that though she had not assimilated it, she was content to be there with him listening to his uncharacteristic babbling. She seemed, even by her silent willingness to listen without taking him too seriously, to be saying "Yes" to him.

"Have you noticed them?" he almost shouted, pointing up with the gesture that the preacher had used more than once that evening. They were standing almost under the canopy now, and it was only because Scriber had seen the glowing faces earlier that he could distinguish one from the other. From that angle they looked much the same, the smile and the grimace, the one now friendly, now mocking, the other first hostile, then compassionate. And had they revolved with the carrousel, they would have coalesced into one expression of benign indifference, or was it that the caricatures of human joy and sorrow, comedy and tragedy, became more human and not so distant as they merged into one visage?

The music began to retard at the cue of some invisible maestro, and the carrousel slowed, the horses becoming more graceful as they slid slowly on the burnished poles until their vertical motion matched exactly their forward speed. They came all at once to what was not so much a final halt as an absolutely motionless suspension, like someone holding his breath and pretending to be dead, frozen now like the faces above, which seemed to mimic both laughter and sorrow.

Two children passed, tugging at their father's hands and doing a small dance that was a delaying action: "Let us do it again, please, Daddy. We don't want to get off. I want to ride the red horse." The young man squatted, took one in each arm and, rising easily, carried them toward a pretty woman who began immediately to shake her head to try to look stern through her smiling.

The horses stood three abreast. Dorie took the middle red one which was now standing high so that Scriber gave her a little boost up to the saddle. His horse was on the outside, its blue head thrown up and out so that Scriber could see one large eye and a half-crescent of teeth. As the music began, the blue horse rose slowly, as Dorie's stallion fell, looking straight ahead, indifferent to the serene face of the riderless white horse on the inside which rose now as slowly as fog, in sequence with Scriber's mount.

Dorie was holding on to the pole, the golden rod sliding through her hands. She began to giggle as the music quickened and the carrousel gathered speed in all its hidden gears and pistons, rising and falling and returning and leaving and returning again.

Scriber sat easily on the blue horse, its large eye fixed on him. It was possible to feel that he was stationary, that the boardwalk and the sea and the tall white cross beyond the lake and the dark high house were rising and falling and coming and going and returning again.

He looked at Dorie. Did she feel in this towering and sinking down, anything more than what was on her face, sheer delight and amusement at him and herself? She rose easily too, and quietly, moving with the elemental motion of a woman who knows in her body, as a man cannot know, the ebb and flow of the tide, the mingling and pleasure and pain of renewing, deep within the unseen recesses of body and mind.

Dorie rode as a woman, and even as they laughed together, Scriber knew that because of her he was here, on this carrousel. He rode now as a new man, and the old one was right there with him. And he thought as he rode that the woman with the Big S and his aunt with her head in her hands, as if resting while praying over breakfast, and Ruthie and the market lady and Todd and Gates, and Miss Shoemaker—that they all rode with him, and with Dorie. And he rode with Addie Belle, and Nina and Abbie, and their hellfire pastor. And Mark and Dot and Oscar were all there grabbing for the brass ring and blending into one.

And the young preacher's words came ringing in his ears, "where can you lose yourself and find yourself at the same time?"

The kingdom of God is now. His long legs could have touched the boards half the time, but he had drawn his feet up into the too-small stirrups and was letting the horse bear him up and down, up and down, in that same elemental rhythm from which he had come, and which he possessed, and which it was so hard for him to give himself up to.

Round and round, the sea and the lake and the tall white bars of the tabernacle's cross, where he had sat alone last night—remembering and fearing and hoping—and where even tonight he had wanted to seize the treasure and run it to some secret, high place and sing out in his own voice what was there but which for so long he had not been able to sing.

Now he rose and fell, his body telling him more than he knew about how it was all one—this woman beside him who for three years had been there, rising and falling, up and down with him—and all those things that had come back new in two days, like the boardwalk and the lake and the sea that kept coming round and round him, and those two bright lines meeting beyond the big old houses where people with their bibles on their bed tables now slept in each other's arms and moved up and down and forward through the night to that final suspension when the faces were frozen and the horses as still as a man and a woman in a field of daisies transfixed before a skittish butterfly, or two young men lying quietly in a shady place listening to the sea and to their hearts. Anyone with eyes to see, watching Scriber Newall and the healthy

young woman beside him, the white horse falling and rising
beyond them, could not have missed knowing that they were
the best of friends and that he was smiling.

The time will come
when, with elation
you will greet yourself arriving
at your own door, in your own mirror
and each will smile at the other's welcome,

and say, sit here. Eat.
You will love again the stranger who was your self.
Give wine. Give bread. Give back your heart
to itself, to the stranger who has loved you

all your life, whom you ignored
for another, who knows you by heart.
Take down the love letters from the bookshelf,

the photographs, the desperate notes,
peel your own image from the mirror.
Sit. Feast on your life.

Made in the USA
Middletown, DE
13 January 2018